Wild Card

A Satirical Business Adventure

Stephen Kirk

Zero Point Publishing

LONDON, ENGLAND

Stephen Kirk/Zero Point Publishing
10 Houblon Road,
Richmond, Surrey TW10 6DE
http://www.stephenkirk.co.uk/

Publisher's Note: This is a work of fiction. Names, characters, places, and incidents are a product of the author's imagination. Locales and public names are sometimes used for atmospheric purposes. Any resemblance to actual people, living or dead, or to businesses, companies, events, institutions, or locales is completely coincidental.

Wild Card/ Stephen Kirk. -- 1st ed.
ISBN: 978-1-0369-1530-8

Dedication

This book is dedicated to my friends and business associates, including my competitors who make life more fun!

Special thanks to Leanda Michelle for her invaluable help in publishing this book. Also to Luiza who encouraged me to finish and publish *Wild Card* for the enjoyment of those who know me… and for those who don't… yet!

"Life is a mystery.
A long dream from which one day we wake!"

–STEPHEN KIRK

Contents

THE ELECTRICITY COMMISSION

1

The Eighties, London...

Early Monday morning, I stroll down Millbank, enter Fuse House, up to The Electricity Commission floor, enter the office.

This morning, nobody's around. In our in-tray, a strange memo; an Honours list of twenty individuals in the electricity supply industry. They do it every year. Who cares?

If anyone deserves a knighthood, it's me.

'Do this for Me,' commands God.

I thrust my head out of the door, survey the corridor. Not a soul. I carefully type a new list on Julie's typewriter, add my name, Sir Richard Stern.

I place the fake in the office in-tray, tear up the original list and throw it in the waste bin.

Never a dull moment in the Electricity Commission! Can I go through with this mad plan? No! I've gone too far—even for me.

I retype the list, add, Ricky Stern CBE. Commander of the British Empire. Sounds more realistic. I'll go to Buck Palace, meet the Queen, what's not to like?

Voices in the corridor! I place the fake memo back in the tray, open my Sainsbury's bag executive briefcase, grab the latest printout, study it.

Suddenly, the office springs into life.

Mousey-haired Julie opens and shuts her metal filing cabinet. She approaches. Wears a dowdy cream blouse, carries a white paper bag. 'Did you eat breakfast today, Ricky?'

I sit at my desk, overlooking the air-conditioning unit, wonder why everyone else has a Thames view, then stare at the computer printout.

'I can't find the fault in this blasted lightning prediction program,' I reply.

'Brought you a Danish,' she says, thrusting me the bag.

'You don't understand, Pete. We shouldn't accept *any* award,' shouts Ted emphatically.

Pete slithers towards Ted, swaying unsteadily. His limp body hangs from a snake's head.

'You f-fuckin' crazy, why the f-fuckin' hell not?' Pete flushes, thick eyebrows arch.

'Well, I was wondering what Jesus might do, in the circumstances?' Ted looks to Heaven, waiting for an answer.

'What's fuckin' Jesus gotta do with it? 'E's fuckin' dead,' continues Pete.

'He'd ask for all the money to be distributed to the poor.' Mutters Ted to himself.

'I *am* the fuckin' poor!'

'You've had three pay awards this year, plus an extra week's holiday Pete.'

'Jesus died 2,000 years ago,' I say. 'I haven't bumped into him on the Tube recently.'

'Shurrup, bloody scabbie!' Pete yells.

'He's not dead to me, Ricky,' Ted replies.

'Nor I,' *saith the Lord*.

Julie drops her biro, rolls her head, yawns, stretches, notices the memo in the in-tray. She strolls across to read it, squeals, 'Ricky Stern, Richard Stern... What *have* you done? Wow! You've gone and got a CBE!'

'What?' I feign surprise.

'Look, here!' She points at my name.

'Oh dear, it was meant to be a secret.'

'Look everyone, Ricky's gotta CBE!' She waves the memo wildly.

I must confess before things get out of hand. Ted dashes over. Pete eyes me with suspicion.

'Gee, *Ricardo*,' Ted shakes my hand, 'well done!'

Own up?

Pete grabs the paper and holds it up to the light. 'You're a fuckin' fraud, laddie!'

'Steady on, Pete. What makes you think that?' asks Ted.

'I know, I just know. So, tell us, Commander Stern. Exactly what did you do to gain this honour?'

Bloody anti-Semite. Jews don't get CBEs, do they, big boy?

'They weren't supposed to announce it yet.'

'You're a shit fraud!' Pete punches the air.

Julie ticks the memo, places it in her out-tray. Soon the messenger will transport it to the next department. Retract it before then? First, keep Pete guessing. I clear myself a space amongst old printouts, empty crisp bags, a snap of Susie, my wife. Begin a new program to predict the number of birds that'll fly into overhead cables? Riveting! After ten minutes, I rise to retrieve the sham memo.

Gone, *disparu, vamooshed.* I dash into the neighbouring office.

'Lost something?' asks the cute IR girl with pert, button nose, cupid lips. Wish I wasn't wearing dirty specs, frayed olive-green cords, scuffed black shoes.

'No, no, nothing in particular.'

'Can we help you?' ask the Accounts pair, involved in an illicit affair. Caught them snogging in St. James Park during lunch break. She returned with a leaf in her hair, grass stains on the back of her skirt.

'No, I'm fine, thanks.'

They giggle.

No sign of the memo in PR, Health and Safety, Technical Services, and Commercial. So, I've given myself a CBE, so what? I deserve a fillip working with these morons. I return to my desk, pick up the prediction formula developed by the Research Department, continue coding. Julie grins at me, her face partially obscured by a giant rubber plant leaf. 'Ricky, did you meet the Queen?'

'Queen?'

'You know, when you received your CBE?'

'Oh, her, no. I mean yes. Yes, of course.'

'Yer don't seem too soddin' sure of yer facts,' scoffs Pete.

'Leave him alone, Pete. You're just jealous!' Julie says.

'Jealous? Of a fuckin' conman?'

The Big Boss, Byron, enters. Straight-backed, avuncular ex-Army. He strides up, thumps me on my back. 'Richard! Congrats! Well done! We'll run an article on you in the *Electron* staff Mag.'

Christ, the Beefeaters'll be after me. Ted and Julie watch with pride. Ravenous tiger Pete stands, arms crossed, waiting to devour me.

'I'm sorry but I'm afraid that won't be possible,' I say.

'Why ever not?' asks Byron.

'Well, it's embarrassing. My award should never have been publicised. It was supposed to have been confidential.'

'Won't you give us a little clue?'

'No, it's not possible.'

'Oh, one of those covert jobbies, eh! I get it. Mum's the word!' Big Boss thumps my shoulder and marches back to his lair on the Executive Floor.

'Despicable liar!' snipes Pete.

'Let him alone. What was she wearing, Ricky?' asks Julie.

'Who?'

'The fuckin' Queen, who else? He doesn't know because he wasn't there, that right, scabbie?' scowls Pete.

'Pink. A pale pink dress, matching shoes, diamond necklace, no crown.' I stutter.

My phone rings. 'Hello, Rick. Ken Smith, Personnel Director, here. Will you please pop along to my office for a chat?'

Jesus Christ, now I'm well and truly fucked!

I ramble along endless corridors. Whole life flashes before me. The Southend Pier miniature railway. Eating a strawberry lolly, getting pneumonia. First kiss, open mouth, like a garage door.

Round a corner, lost in thought, bump into a thin engineer. He smells of sweat.

'You finished the lightnin' program yet?'

'This afternoon,' I reply. He rushes on.

Eventually, reach the Executive Centre. Commander Stern bites the dust.

Ken Smith, Personnel Director, a small owlish man with thinning silver hair, sidles to the door to greet me. His face drops as he eyes my T-shirt and cords. 'Please come in,' and closes the door.

He motions me to sit in a brown armchair. Two cups of tea and a plate of Digestives rest on a coffee table. I glance at his wall photos, nuke power stations, birdwatching group, Ken with his arm around Mrs Ken.

'Forgive me asking, but are you in disguise?' Obviously shocked by my *schlock-look*.

'No.' I reach for the phantom top button of my T-shirt. He bites a biscuit, wipes crumbs off his brown suit jacket, clears his throat. 'I hear you don't want publicity.'

I protest but he raises his hand to block me. 'It's all right, Byron's explained.'

Can you believe it? He actually believes I've got a CBE.

He takes a deep breath. 'Look, we know you're not entirely happy here, but we really do appreciate your efforts. We're looking to promote you to management but this union business is getting in the way.' He throws me a comradely smile. 'Could you see a way to rejoin?'

'Hmm...'

We sit facing a sweeping view of The Thames. Rain beats against the windowpanes. Below, pedestrians fight with umbrellas as they approach Fuse House.

'I resigned because the Union Executive ignored a democratic vote to accept the pay offer,' says Commander Stern, a political activist.

'I know all that but we're a closed shop. As it stands, we're compelled to fire you.'

'Then the Union will strike.' What a fiasco!

'Things are changing. I'm on your side. It's only a matter of time, old boy.' Says Ken.

'I don't follow.'

He leans forward, whispers, 'Tea?'

'No, thanks. I haven't finished this cup.'

He sighs, exasperated. 'Mrs T.' Oh, Mrs T *Zieg Heil*! 'If you were to rejoin...' He taps his armrest.

And what about my principles? I'd have to compromise for promotion.

'Ok.' I stretch out my legs and sink into my armchair.

He leans back in sympathy, exhales deeply. 'Good lad! Now, is there anything we can do to make your life more interesting?'

What an offer! Weekend visit to NW Electric, Chester with the IR girl? I'm married, too complicated. Pete garrotted? That's illegal. 'I've always dreamed of travelling on business.'

'Leave it to me.'

Where will he send me? The fault management centre at Oswestry? Exciting...

Back in my office Julie waves a bright red plastic watering can over her sickly cyclamen.

'Baby's poorly, it's the air.' She scowls up at the ceiling air-conditioner. 'Please sing to him, Ricky? Sing, he likes baritones.'

'What shall I sing?'

'I've grown accustomed to your face. His favourite.'

Pete, head down over a coding sheet, mutters, 'Jesus!'

I pull my chair near to Julie's, and croon the nostalgic song over the plant. Ted joins, loudly and off-key.

'For fuck's sake!' yells Pete. Two books sail over my head and land by my feet.

'That'll do,' says Julie, 'He doesn't like aggression!' She glares at Pete.

I place *The Communist Manifesto* and *Mao's Little Red Book*, on top of Pete's Union Handbook. I pull my chair over to Pete and sit beside him.

'Clear off, scab.'

'Calm down.' I admire his red-checked lumberjack shirt, Doc Martens, newly cut and washed brown hair. I pat his arm but he whisks it away. 'Don't touch me, I might catch something nasty.'

Charming. 'I want to rejoin the Union.'

'Oh?' He throws his head back, honks. 'This wouldn't have anything to do with your con trick, would it?'

Typical! Commander Stern approaches the enemy with an olive branch and gets shit thrown in his face. 'I acted hastily, I regret it, I'm sorry.'

'Oh, sweet.' Julie's speaking to her cyclamen as she gazes at me absent-mindedly.

'Gee, Pete,' shouts Ted, 'that's very gracious of our Ricky.'

Pete opens his right-hand drawer and pulls out a form, 'I guess you're up to something, as per usual. Nothing's straightforward with you.' He thrusts me a Union Membership application form.

Dungeness nuclear power station, here we come!

Next morning, before I've taken off my bomber jacket, Ken calls and beckons me into his office. Throw my jacket onto the coat stand, then bound along with a spring in my step. He waits by his door, smart casual. Brown suit, tie with bright red stripe, top shirt button undone.

I've even made a sartorial effort. Open-necked green cotton shirt, formal grey trousers, polished black shoes, combed hair.

As we sit, he says, 'Ricky, good news.' My heart leaps. 'There's an international conference of Electricity high-fliers – The Live Wires.' He pours us both tea, offers me a Chocolate Digestive.

'Where?'

'Frankfurt?'

I choke on my Digestive, 'Is this a sick joke?'

His hurt face falls. 'I thought you'd be pleased. It takes place every three years. We'd like you to be one of our two UK reps.'

'What's the problem?' Ken stares at my contorted face.

'It'll upset my father.'

'Why might that be?' His compassionate eyes show concern.

'We're Jewish.'

'Oh, I see. Why's that a problem when it was a helluva long time ago that...?'

'Not to my father.'

'There'll be delegates from all over the world. Germany's only hosting the conference.'

'Who's the other UK rep?'

'My son, Don. He's a graduate sales trainee at the Lewisham Electricity Showroom.' The Lewisham Electricity Showroom! And I thought my job was pathetic.

'Your kid?'

His cup freezes halfway to his lips, 'Yep, what 'bout it?'

'Won't folks be suspicious?'

His face darkens, eyes narrow, frown deepens. 'What folks? Nobody knows how you got your CBE, do they?' He looks directly into my eyes.

God whispers, *'He is an angel in the guise of Man.'*

He gulps his tea, 'There you go, then.' He places his cup on a saucer, sits back, hands behind his head, stares at the ceiling. 'The Electricity Industry needs more people like you, Richard. People with initiative.'

'Thanks, Ken.'

'Ricky, don't take this personally, but you'll have to smarten yourself up. You'll be representing *Grande Bretagne*, remember.'

My special effort obviously wasn't good enough!

"Bye then.' He rises as he wolfs the last biscuit.

Bugger off Stern, your time's up. Off to Deutschland, with you me lad.

How *will* I tell Dad?

2

Susie and I travel to Edgware by Tube for Sunday afternoon tea with my parents. Mum shepherds us to the dining table. Dad sits hunched in his armchair watching an Arsenal match on TV.

'Samuele, enough already!' shouts Mum.

Dad shuffles over to join us, an angry bear.

Susie sits demurely. Fringed, fair hair, freckled skin, floral cotton dress, Greek sandals. She spots her opportunity. 'Ricky's got something to tell you, Ma and Pa.'

'*Oi gevalt!* You've lost your job?' shouts Mum.

Dad eyes smoked salmon sandwiches, bagels, chocolate cake and Swiss Roll. Crumbs decorate his navy jumper.

'Not exactly...' Susie warned me that I couldn't visit Germany secretly, that I'd have to be honest. 'I'm being sent to an international Electricity Industry Conference, representing the UK – in Frankfurt.'

Silence.

Dad thumps the table, 'Germany? Nation of Murderers!' Tea slops from my cup into the china saucer.

'You should be ashamed of yourself!' says Mum, unhelpfully. She grabs Dad's arm. 'What will we tell everyone, Samuele?' A petite redhead in a blue summer dress, matching red shoes, she's a budding amateur artist.

Hope they won't write a letter to *The Jewish Chronicle* disowning me.

Susie dabs her mouth with a paper napkin. 'There'll be people from countries all over the world,' she says. Their faces soften.

Susie bites into a smoked salmon bagel. Lips coated with cream cheese.

'How long will you be there?' asks Dad, grumpily.

'Two days, stuck in an airport hotel. Hardly see any Krauts. I promise I won't talk to anyone over fifty.' Susie kicks me under the table, Dad grimaces.

'And there's the other thing, isn't there Ricky, dear?' Susie says. Married to a truth serum. Launch into confession of my forgery. Omit God's part in the affair.

'Amazing! They really believe you've gotta CBE?' asks Mum.

'Yep.'

'*Mazeltov!* That's the Stern way,' says Dad.

'I think he should own up,' says a baffled Susie.

'What, and spoil the fun?' says my hunched Dad. Balding curly grey-haired gnome. I have inherited his lack of dress sense. 'You keep *schtum*, son. Grandpa Hymie would have given himself a knighthood. Stuff the lot of 'em.' He pats my knee.

Susie's crestfallen, poor girl. Hasn't bargained on marrying into a family of tricksters.

Dad regales us with anecdotes about Mr Aziz who swallowed his gold inlay; the woman who spat mouthwash in his face; the man who filled his own tooth with Toothypegs and couldn't close his mouth.

As we leave, Mum coos, '*Nachus*, my son the CBE!'

Prepare for the conference. Get my hair cut. Buy a smart Italian suit and Crombie coat. On the Big Day, travel by Tube to Heathrow Terminal 2, with my new briefcase and proceed through Departures to the gate.

Ken's son, Don has been assigned the aisle seat next to mine. Keep a lookout for him. Is he the suave public schoolboy reading, *The Financial Times*, ahead of me in the boarding queue?

Settle into my Lufthansa Business Class seat. Billy Bunter tries to sit beside me. Creased Prince of Wales suit, school tie.

'I'm sorry, this seat's reserved...'

'For me, Don Smith. Hello, old bean. Dad told me all about you.' Perspiring heavily, he addresses the entire plane. 'Some of my best friends are Jews.' *Oi Vey*!

'Chop Chop!' Lowers his arm abruptly and I shake his hand. His huge leather satchel is stuffed with conference papers. He shoves it under his seat.

'I intend to screw as many gals as possible in Frankfurt.' He swigs champagne, pretzels, crisps. After the snack, he presses the stewardess call button. 'Anything else edible, *Fraulein*?' The stewardess finds him a ham roll. He guzzles beer, spills it on his paunch, burps loudly. 'Funny, you being the only Jew in the Commission.'

'Why?'

'I thought you lot always stuck together...'

He staggers to the toilet, too pissed to shut the door properly. He stands, member in hand.

'Don! Shut the door.' He can't hear me. 'Don!' I walk to the toilet.

'You pervert, what you doin' here?' he yells.

'You left the door open.'

'Wondered who all those folks were.' He points at the reflections in the mirror.

He returns to his seat, passes out, snores heavily, leans against my shoulder, farts.

The stewardess kneels, whispers, 'Iz zis man bothering you?'

'He's a colleague.'

'Poor you. More orange juice?'

Don's face lights up as we pass Hiller Bookshop in the airport Arrivals lounge. He goose-steps towards Customs, points at me, shouts, 'This way, Rick. Better hide those Durex.'

The conference is a two-day affair at a faceless hotel on the airport perimeter. My badge reads: Richard Stern CBE. 200 delegates from 60 countries, arranged in rows behind long tables. Sip Evian, suck a mint, doodle with pencil, read the agenda.

The first day's topics include such stimulating subjects as:

Is Nuclear Energy Safe?

Fault Reporting in the 21st Century

Electricity supply in the Gobi Desert

Everything's in English. Stick my headphones into a socket and listen to simultaneous translations into European, Middle Eastern and Asian languages. Part of a super electric family.

On the second day, we split into groups. Mine prepares a presentation on 'Making The Electric Industry An Attractive Career Option.' Fifteen members sit around a conference table and elect Leader, Holly, a smart Hong Kong girl.

She whips us into shape, scrawls on the overhead projector, 'The Electricity Industry is young, vital and dynamic...'

Which planet are they on?

At the Conference Farewell Dinner, I sit next to Holly. She wears a turquoise silk dress, matching high-heels, and silver jewellery. As if she's at the Oscars.

'Great presentation,' I say.

'Thanks,' Chinese-American accent.

'Do you honestly believe all that stuff you presented?'

'Sure, I do. In a few years, Hong Kong will be returned to China. China needs to produce energy efficiently. I'll be able to advise on all the new technologies... and the old ones, traditional, nuclear, wind, you name it.' I ponder. 'That's the problem with you Brits, you only look back. Our excitement is yet to come. By the way, what's the CBE on your badge stand for?'

'Can't Beat Electric,' I reply.

'Oh, very good.' She makes a note on her pad.

On my way to bed, I pass the bar. Don's holding court. Booze, fags, crisps, peanuts are scattered everywhere. He lounges on a sofa with a black girl on each arm. An Oriental girl stretched across his fat legs, strokes his hair.

'Moses, come 'ere! Can't 'andle 'em all on me own.'

'No, thanks. I'm off to bed.' Alone.

'Too bad. This one,' an Indian girl, 'has a thing about circumcised men.'

Back in the office, Julie says, 'Ricky, you look like James Bond!' I'm dressed in my posh suit. Tasted the high life.

'007 in person.' Pete stops mid-sentence.

Ken Smith hovers in the doorway. He beckons me to follow him. 'A word?' he says.

As we approach his office, he says, 'Had an early meeting in IR. Thought I'd pick you up on the way back.'

He stands behind his desk, sorts his post, assigns each opened letter to: In, Out or Pending. I sit in the visitor's chair and wait. Eventually, he lowers himself slowly into his brown upright chair. 'Back trouble,' he complains. 'How did you get on at the conference?'

'I enjoyed it.'

'Top form.' He brightens.

'And Don?'

He's an ogre. Coarse, rude, vulgar. 'Tremendous fun,' I reply.

'Thought you'd be on the same wavelength. Listen,' he leans forward, his clasped hands resting on the desk, 'there's a chance for you two to work together.'

Kill me. Do it now. 'Really?'

'Look Ricky, I have friends in, well how can I put this... high places... and they are always asking to let them know if I spot any rising stars.'

'And?'

'Well, the Government is setting up GRAPE, a special company to sell software overseas and I'm recommending they look you over.

'Can I have a Thames view?'

'Thames-view? You'd not be based here! You'd be based in Holborn.'

Curious and curiouser.

And why on Earth name a company after a fruit? Ridiculous!

GRAPE

3

GRAPE occupies three floors of a converted townhouse in Lincoln's Inn Fields. Dolly bird on Reception takes me straight into George Langton.

He shakes my hand, asks, 'Are you a Mason?'

Wouldn't he know from the handshake?

'No...' I reply.

He's tall, wears a handmade black suit, a red tie and a moustache. His cosy office overlooks Lincoln's Inn Fields. Large plasticised wall chart of the World. Desk clear, save for a GRAPE memo. His black leather briefcase stands in the corner by his tightly rolled, black umbrella.

His eye twitches. A Masonic sign? 'Not to worry, we'll sort that out later. I gather you're an EC High Flyer.'

'Apparently.'

'Don't be modest!' he laughs, 'Ken says you know how to handle yourself. We're recruiting four salesmen. Two will be experienced; then there'll be two apprentices. Don Smith will be one, of course.'

'Of course?' I reply.

'He's one of us.' One of what? 'You could be the other.'

'What does the job involve?' Don't want to be a Mason with a handkerchief tied round my knee.

'You'll sell our revolutionary two-way communications systems using something called internet...'

'Into-what?' I ask.

'In-*ter*-net. It will transform communications. Obviously, there'll be lots of travel. Interested?'

'Travel?' I interrupt him mid-flow.

'Oh yes, forgot to mention. We have a worldwide licence, except for the UK. British Embassies will feed you leads.'

Never thought a CBE would make such a difference. Should have granted myself a knighthood after all. That'll teach me to have scruples.

'I'm gob-smacked.'

He smiles in a fraternal, Masonic fashion.

'That's settled then. Starting salary's twenty-five grand. I trust that'll be sufficient?' I nod, being currently on seventeen. 'Ken says he'll arrange your transfer for six weeks' time. He'll break the news to your boss this afternoon....'

'Oh, one last question... What's GRAPE stand for?'

'Haven't a fucking clue,' replies George. 'Some marketing idiot. I mean who'd name a company after a fruit?'

'And what exactly will I be selling?'

George looks flustered.

'Don't worry, Don will fill you in.'

'And why not the UK?' I continue my interrogation.

'You ask too many questions, young man. Don will tell you everything you need to know...'

Stroll back to Fuse House, through the rubble of the Covent Garden Market reconstruction, bustling Leicester Square, grand houses of Parliament. Who'll finish my current program? Prediction of suicide by electricity. Who'll sit in my seat? Ken Smith's cousin?

Enter my office, take up position by the Teletype plinth, clear throat, 'Excuse me, I have an announcement.'

Pete gives me a V-sign, continues working. Julie swings her chair round. Ted lays down his biro, sits bolt upright. 'I'm leaving in six weeks,' I announce.

Pete throws his biro in the air, shouts, 'Yeah!'

'Grow up, Pete,' shouts Ted. He wears his standard green cardy, white shirt, fawn carpet slippers.

'Leaving?' Julie's eyes moisten. I'm distracted by her straightened dyed blond hair, red gypsy décolleté top, long green dress, matching moon boots. Must have a new boyfriend.

'I'm transferring to a new Government company.... called GRAPE.'

'GRAPE?' scoff's Pete. 'What sort of a poncey name is that?'

I ignore the question. Partly, because I agree with him.

'What floor?' asks Ted.

'It's in Holborn.'

'That's not far enough for me!' smirks Pete.

'Sod off!' I reply.

Julie rushes over to hug me, 'I'll miss you.' I prise her off and shake Ted's hand.

Pete swaggers over, says, 'I'll miss you too, Jimmy.' He crushes me inside his leather jacket with a bear hug. He loves me after all.

In the middle of this touching parting scene, big boss Byron enters and salutes. 'Farewell, Commander Stern.' About time I was shown some respect.

Six weeks later, Don and I are ensconced on the mezzanine floor near Reception. Four desks are arranged classroom style. He's claimed the back right one, in front of the door, beside a wall noticeboard. He busies himself unpacking his satchel, pins up family snaps, places a large blue diary on his desk, together with a penholder and index card box.

'Ready for battle!' He declares.

I settle, back left by the open balcony exit, doodle on a notepad. My only belonging is a calculator. Left my coding sheets, pencils and erasers behind.

We reserve the front two desks for George's experienced heavy hitters. They start next week.

Don's phone rings. 'Yeah, Right!' He slams the receiver down.

'Come on, Solomon. George wants a pow-wow.'

He shoots out with me in hot pursuit.

George's Hong Kong, hand-made, Masonic suit flatters his thin frame. He dabs his forehead with a white linen handkerchief, says, 'Bit of a problem on the recruitment front. You two'll be running the whole show until we get re-enforcements. Think you can hack it?' His right eye twitches.

'Your guys not coming?' I ask.

'No,' he replies, sheepishly.

I'll be running the asylum, with Don, a quasi-lunatic!

'Leave it to us.' says Don.

'I've every confidence.' George's clean-shaven face perspires. A bead of sweat rests on his moustache. There's been a mega cock-up!

Don and I return to our bunker up a small staircase. We step onto our balcony and survey the human zoo below. Lincoln's Inn Fields provides a home for the homeless. A cardboard city, encircled by barbed wire. The inmates huddle in groups carousing.

'I'd shoot the lot of 'em if I was King!' mumbles Don, chomping nicotine chewing gum.

'What's going on?' I ask.

'Talked it through with George over a round of golf.' Weekend trysts with George? 'Between you and me, he's made a complete balls-up. The two blokes he had in the frame have abandoned ship.'

'Why so?'

'Need you ask, Samson? George's a bear of little brain. He only got the gig 'cos he attends the same club as Sir Ramsey, GRAPE Chairman. Anyway, Georgie will be retiring soon. Those new blokes checked him out. Didn't like what they saw. Couldn't contemplate working for him. Pulled out an hour before contract signature.'

'Why their sudden change of heart?'

'I had lunch with 'em....' He winks. 'I showed 'em press cuttings. Show you, if you like?'

Machievelli pops back into the office and returns with two photostats. One is a short report from the FT. A year ago, George was dismissed from his last post. The other is a Private Eye article which insinuates that George is a reckless gambler.

'So why are *you* staying?' I ask.

'Where's your innate cunning? I was selling washing machines in Lewisham. Then Dad arranges for me to work for a wanker, travel the world and bonk away! There's only one way, Shylock—up! Now we don't have anyone to report to, 'cept Georgey-Porgey, and he doesn't count. We're masters of all we survey.' He gestures across squatters in the Fields.

'A land of milk and honey? Let my people go!' says God'

We're assigned a Sloany seccie, Vanessa Hardon in a skimpy frock. She speaks like the Queen, chain-smokes. Life treats her badly. Haunted, sallow, mousy hair, bruises on her arm. She sits at the bottom of our stairs, awaiting orders.

On Monday morning, Bonaparte formulates a battle plan. He's moved himself to the front right desk.

Vanessa places a coffee pot and plastic cups on the spare desk and sits. Drag my chair next to hers to pour myself a coffee.

Don pins a rough hand drawn paper map of Europe to the wall. He stands to address his troops, chomps on a croissant, speaks mouth-full, 'This internet thing will revolutionise communications. Europe needs us. You, Einstein, take North; I'll take South.' Draws a line through the middle of the blob.

'You get Scandinavia, Holland, Belgium, Germany, Switzerland; I get Italy, Greece, Spain and Portugal, France.' He writes the name of each country roughly under his name or mine.

'Give me a break Don. Swap Germany for Italy.'

'Why on Earth would I do that Groucho?!'

'You bloody well know why Don, give me a break...'

'I nose what you mean.' He touches his nose, does a Hitler salute and goosesteps. 'But no deal!'

'I've had enough of this shit.' I tear the word Germany from under my name and eat it!

Vanessa screams.

I chew the paper. It has an acidity taste... and swallow.

Don smiles and claps, 'Worthy of Shakespeare! Bravo, bravo. Don't want you to have a breakdown before we've even begun our mission. Out of the kindness of my heart, I'll swap Italy for Germany. But don't fuck it up...'

Jesus that was a close shave.

'You're welcome,' says a strange voice in my head.

'Van, I want you to contact the British Embassy in each territory. Ask for the Commercial Attaché. If anyone asks, you're working for GRAPE, a Government Agency. Got it?' orders Don.

Vanessa looks vague. 'Err, where do I find Embassy telephone numbers?'

Don gives her a withering look. 'From the Foreign Office, sweetheart. Didn't they teach you anything at Finishing School?'

'Sorry, Don, wasn't thinking.' She blushes and departs.

'We'll launch our attack in October,' says Don. 'It'll give Vanessa a chance to get marketing materials sorted.'

Can't wait!

One afternoon, whilst waiting for our battle plan to commence I skive off to see my old comrades at the Commission.

Ted's in full flow.

'Sydney's the most wonderful place on Earth. No crime. Beautiful harbour.'

'Why don't you go back there,' yells Pete.

Julie is marking up a printout. I say, 'Morning, campers.' She swivels round. 'Ricky! Stranger!'

'Gee, Ricky, what brings you here?' Ted hobbles to greet me.

Julie darts over, 'You *must* see something!' She leads me by the hand to her desk. A stone rests in a straw basket, between two diminutive cacti. 'What do you think, isn't he lovely?'

I'm lost for words. It's a stone.

'He's my pet rock, I christened him yesterday. Guess his name.'

'Ricky?'

'Who told you? Him?' She points at Pete.

'I worked it out for myself.'

'Like to stroke him?' She rubs her forefinger over the stone's belly.

'No, thanks, I'll pass.' Mad, but harmless. Unlike Don. I sit on my old desk and tell them of my glorious prospects. Travels, pay rise, infinite expenses. 'Only problem, I'm working with an anti-Semite and a degenerate Mason.'

'You can't have everything, Rick.' says Ted, 'After all Jesus died for all Mankind. Perhaps it's time to bring Him into your life, wed yourself to Him.'

'Thanks Ted, we'd need a king-sized bed.'

Enough already!... Back to GRAPE.

4

'I thought I'd split Europe between you both,' says George. George has hijacked Don's idea!

'Marvellous!' replies lapdog Don.

'Ricky, you have Northern Europe: Scandinavia, the Low Countries and France. Knowing how much you love Germany, I'll give it to Don. You can have Italy in return.'

He's a brainwashed puppet with Don pulling the strings.

'Thanks, George.' I reply.

'And Donald, you have Southern Europe: Spain, Portugal, Greece and...'

‘Monaco.’ Don, makes a land grab for hot countries.

‘Monaco. Good thinking.’

‘And South Africa, George?’ asks Don.

‘That’s not Europe.’ I interject. Don scowls.

‘Someone’s gotta have it.’ He stares wide-eyed at George.

‘Have South Africa,’ says George, ‘I’ll do the States. We’ve appointed agents for the other territories.’

‘Brilliant, George-pie. Top gun.’

‘Thanks, Don.’

George walks proudly round his desk. We shake hands. ‘Chop! Chop! Chop!’

‘By the way boys, I’ve put additional recruitment on hold. If we can keep overheads down, it’ll mean there’ll be a bigger bonus pool for us all!’

‘Very smart, George,’ I say.

Don swaggers back to our bunker. I skulk behind him. Hear my phone, but Don’s ahead of me. He grabs the receiver, bellows, ‘Weapons Procurement,’ squats on the floor. His fat face with owlish specs hovers above my desktop.

‘Give it to me!’ I hiss trying to wrestle the receiver from his clutches. He grabs the cradle, sits on his desk, legs sprawled, continues talking. ‘Yeah, that’s right.’ Hear the high pitch of a hysterical woman. ‘That what he told you? No, he’s an arms dealer…’ He pokes his nicotine-stained tongue at me. 'I know… I know…' What does he bloody know?

Grab a pad, scrawl *Who is it?* in red biro, place the pad on his lap. He takes the pen and writes, *Your MUM!*

Lunge for the receiver, but the circus lion jerks his wily head, asks, 'Is there a message I can give him? He's currently signing a humungous contract with Saudi Arabia but he shouldn't be long.'

Again, he listens as Mum babbles on.

Don's fat lips droop. The sad lion's a clown. 'Oh, you must be devastated…'

Kneel between his legs, peer into his face and mouth, 'What?'

He raises his free hand to signal patience, says to Mum, 'Nevertheless, it's always a shock… Yes, I'll tell him.' He scrawls on my pad: *Grandpa pegged it. Funeral Waltham Abbey 3pm TODAY!*

Bloody hell! Grandpa Hymie's performed his final card trick. Jewish funerals should take place the same day if possible otherwise the body has to be watched all night until the funeral next day.

I recall Grandpa Hymie's wry smile when we wheeled him into the Hospice, and he saw its name: The De'ath Memorial Hospital, Finchley.

No time to wallow. How do I get to Waltham Abbey? Tube to Manor House, grab a taxi. Alternatively…

'My name? Don... Don Smith-Berg!' Don stresses *Berg* with a poor imitation of the Artful Dodger.

Mum prattles on. Don replies, 'Yes, I'd love to. Where?' He takes his fag pack, scribbles on it. 'Ricky will be delighted, we're very close, you know.' He replaces the receiver, dumps the phone back on the desk, smiles a beautific Cheshire cat smile.

'You bugger!' I shout.

He grins mischievously. 'You'd better beetle off to Waltham Abbey before the body gets cold. That why they call it a *shiver*?'

'Shiva? That'll be tonight. The funeral's at Waltham Abbey Jewish Cemetery. How do you know about *Shivas?'*

He staggers to his feet, brushes down his crumpled grey-striped trousers, falls back into his chair with a thud, 'Cos your Ma just invited me!'

Tell me it's not true. 'Invited *you*! Has she gone mad?'

He shoves his fag pack towards me, indicates my parents' Golders Green address. 'This North London?'

'Don't worry, I'll make an excuse, say you had to shoot off to Moscow to re-arm the Commie Bloc.'

'Do I have to wear special clothes?'

'A head covering,' I snarl.

He looks at his watch theatrically, 'Hadn't you better get a move on? Isn't Waltham Abbey in the sticks?'

I glance at my watch. Only two hours to get to the back of beyond.

Fancy Mum inviting this shithead to the *shiva!*

Evening prayers are ending. At the back of the room, a huge man in a butterfly hat and safari suit, pushes his way towards us. Oh no, it's Don. His head narrowly misses the glass chandelier. Dad slumps in a low *Shiva* chair, surrounded by his fans: Auntie Hetty, Uncle Monty and Gertie.

Don charges like a bull. 'Don't bother to stand up!' he yells.

The room goes quiet. Relatives and friends stare at the flamboyant stranger. 'Chop!'

Dad says, '...and Hymie tap-danced around South America.'

'This your *Pappa?'* Don points at Dad. He scowls. It's a sin to interrupt Dad.

'This is my new colleague, Don,' I explain.

Don leans down, thrusts out huge hand, 'Hello, old fellow. Sorry and all that about the deceased. Chop!'

'Chop?' Dad extends a begrudging paw.

'Chop, Chop!' repeats Don, shaking Dad's hand.

Dad's disdain is palpable. 'Get this moron away from me,' he mutters to me.

Mum appears from nowhere. She's managed to squeeze in a perm between the funeral and *Shiva*. She wears a plain black cotton dress. Her short, red hair is stiff like candy floss.

'Mr Smithberg, pleased to meet you. We spoke on the phone. I'm Rita Stern.'

He bends, shakes her tiny hand. 'Charmed... And condolences to you and your family.' He glances round regally.

Mum blushes, pulls my arm and hisses, 'I hear you're sellin' arms to Arabs! Traitor!' She heads off to the kitchen to serve grub.

Uncle Ben sits next to Dad. He's Dad's brother. Ben's own groupies crouch round in a semi-circle. Don waits for an introduction, points in Ben's direction. I rise from my seat beside Dad and tap Ben's shoulder.

'Want something, Richard?' Uncle Ben asks.

'I'd like to introduce my workmate, Don Smith. He wants to wish you a long life.'

Uncle Ben's darker, broodier, more hunched than Dad. Natty Mafia suit and tie, compared to Dad's *schlock* casual loose black trousers, blue open-necked shirt, brown cardigan.

I signal to Don. He grabs a herring with his claw from a Ladies' Guild waitress, chomps, lowers his hand through the group towards Uncle Ben. 'Chop!' he says.

'Chop?' asks Uncle Ben. He looks at me in disgust, waiting for Don to utter the customary blessing.

'Wish him long life,' I whisper to Don.

A confused Don looks at Ben, then me, and back again.

'Wish him long life,' I hiss.

Don sings operatically, 'Long Life!'

Uncle Ben mutters, 'Imbecile.'

Don inspects mementos on the sideboard. I tap his hand when he tries to lift the white cloth covering family photos. 'What you hiding under there?' he asks.

'Shut up! It's a mark of respect. Behave!' I retort.

He beckons Mum, 'I'm parched, any chance of a cuppa char? Any more grub?'

'What would you like Mr Smithberg? A bagel?' she asks. 'We got smoked salmon an' cream cheese.'

She rushes off and returns with a huge mound of bagels. Don grabs the whole plate. He spots a spare *Shiva* chair hidden in a corner. Lifts it and plonks himself next to Dad. The seat buckles under his weight.

He spits, mouth full of bagel. Mum offers him a white, rose-coloured, china teacup and saucer. Don places his bagel plate under his seat, grabs cup and saucer, slurps tea. He licks his thick lips and shuts his eyes.

What have I done in my past life to be saddled with this monster?

'The sins of thy forbears shall visit you unto the present moment,' saith the Lord.

'Come,' says Don, 'We need to discuss our trip.' He rises and beckons me towards the food table, bagel plate in hand, 'After *Italia.*'

'Italy? She's mine, we agreed.' He's using the *shiva* to nick Italy back!

'George has agreed. We'll present jointly in *Roma*, then I'll attack Berlin.'

A wizened stranger enters in a camel coat, greets Don. 'I'm Nat. I grew up with Richard's father.'

'In Whitechapel?' asks Don.

'Who's this *schlemiel?*' whispers Nat to me.

'Don's a visitor,' I explain.

Nat stares at Don confused. 'Excuse me.... Good to meet you, Don.' Nat extends his hand. 'And you too, old buddy... Chop!' Nat sits next to Dad, staring malevolently at Don. Gives me a, 'what a cretin look.'

Don's NOT coming to another *Shiva*!

5

We hover over Rome airport. I check my horoscope in the In-flight mag. *Time for a change of scenery. An old friend will reappear. Lucky in love.*

'What's your sign, Don?'

'Don't tell me you believe that baloney!' His bulky frame oozes over the armrest and squashes me against the window.

'What's your sign?'

'No idea. Load of drivel.' He picks up a *Telegraph* from under his seat, stares at the front page. *Government Bans Closed Shop Agreements.*

I smile. 'Born late August. I'm a Virgo. And you?'

Doesn't make eye contact. Fumbles for nicotine chewing gum from his breast pocket, stuffs a tab in his mouth.

'March 13th if you must know,' he replies, sullenly chewing.

'You're a Pisces! Never have thought it. *You're a fish out of water. Keep a close eye on expenditure. You can't have your cake and eat it.* That makes sense.'

The plane bumps down onto tarmac. Don accidentally drops his passport onto my lap.

'Let's have a dekker at your photo.'

'Give it back!' He tries to grab his passport.

I dangle it over the aisle.

'Can't you remember your own birthday? Your passport says April 25th. You're a Taurus.' He snatches the passport from me. 'You should have your eyes tested.'

He stuffs his passport in his inside jacket pocket. Sweats profusely.

Taurus. A colleague steals your thunder. Friends in high places. Someone finds you attractive.

We swelter in the back of our stationary taxi. Palm trees sway in the breeze. Elegant Italians stroll and chatter in curbside cafes. The driver cranes forward, eyeing up women. Leans over sideways, sticks his hand out of the side window, addresses a passing comrade.

'Bloody Ities. It'll take hours to get to the Embassy. Don't you know a quicker route, driver?' yells Don. No reply. 'You *spraken Inglese?*'

'No, Signore.'

I pray to the Virgin Mary stuck to the driver's dashboard: *Please protect me from Don this Philistine.*

'Thou Shalt have no Other God but Me. For I am a Jealous God!'

Don sprawls across the backseat, tie and jacket slung over the front passenger seat. He kicks his shoes off, stretches out his legs to reveal holey socks.

'Do you speak any foreign languages, Don?'

'No need, old buddy. Watch this.' He grabs his jacket, extracts his leather wallet, finds 100,000 lire note, dangles it in front of the driver's eyes.

'You get us there *pronto* and this for you, *comprendo?'*

'Si, si!' The driver reaches for the cash.

Don withdraws the notes, snaps wallet shut, says, 'Not so *fasta, amigo*!'

The taxi veers down a side-turning, narrowly missing a Vespa. We hurtle through ancient squares and tiny, narrow roads.

'See, I speak ze lingo, even if I don't speak their bloody language!' Don bellows. 'Now to business... Van and I've been slogging away setting up this week. To-night, you and I'll test the waters, then split. Here's your schedule.' He passes me a folder. 'We start in *Roma*. Embassy staff are superb, mediocre in Paris and Brus-sels. Hague geezer's pleasant but ineffectual. They're out to lunch in Stockholm.'

Glance through my papers. 'How very professional.'

'Van's been a star. Told her to take the rest of the week off. Nothing much for her to do, what with us travelling.' Shifty look. 'You'll see I'm in Berlin tomor-row. Then Athens, Lisbon, working weekend in Monaco, two days Cape Town.'

I commiserate. All that sunshine and sex.

We hurtle down *Via XX Settembre*. Then the Embassy looms ahead. A spaceship on stilts. Modern design by Basil Spence. It's almost attractive.

The taxi stops outside the tradesman's entrance. Don thrusts 150,000 lire into the driver's hand.

'Mille grazie, Signor.' The driver jumps out, opens our door and the boot. He rushes into the Embassy with our bags. Don lurches into Reception, creased jacket over shoulder, tie strung loose around neck.

We push our luggage through an X-ray machine, glide through a metal detector, manned by a handsome Italian guard. An English Rose tells us to sit in the holding area while she makes a call.

A smart thin man with a straight back appears from the lift. Thinning auburn hair, sharp diplomatic suit. 'Greetings, I'm Ashley Goodwin, Commercial Attaché. Let's leave your luggage here.' He dumps our cases next to the English Rose.

'You two gentlemen are the most exciting thing that's happened all year. Your average Brit doesn't set foot outside Old Blighty. Sure, we get the occasional fur trader or gunrunner. The Ambassador wants to say hello.'

Ashley leads us to the ceremonial entrance, then up a magnificent marble staircase, lit by a chandelier Mum would die for. He begins his *spiel*, 'Original Embassy bombed 1946... Basil Spence... completed 1971... two pools... Henry Moore bronze...' My name is Bond. Ricky Bond. Ricky Bond CBE. Shaken and stirred. 'Finally, our ambassador's office.'

A desk-bound spinster with a miserable face confronts us. Polka-dot cotton dress, blue-rinse, huge pointy spectacles.

'Is Sir Ronald in, Martha?' Ashley asks.

'He's busy...' She barely glances up.

A voice booms from the office, 'Come in, Gentlemen! *Bienvenuto in Italia!* I'm Ronald Argyll.' He stands in front of a carved wooden desk under a huge oil painting of Her Majesty. His office is a hot-potch of antiques and sturdy British-designed office chairs. The fax machine enjoys a magnificent view of gardens below.

'Sir Ronald, these two gentlemen...'

'You're Ken Smith's youngest son... Don, isn't it? Chop!' He extends a miniscule arm from his pinstriped suit. Ashley's face turns from red to white.

Don bends down, says, 'Chop!' nods wildly.

'Your father and I were chums in the Royal Signals.' He turns to inspect me. 'And you are?'

'Richard Stern, Sir Rodney.'

Rigorous hand grind, but no 'Chop.'

There's a sudden ear-piercing siren. A glass partition shoots out and separates us from Martha.

Sir Rodney stands proudly in front of his desk, legs apart, hands behind back, 'Impressive, huh? Our very own Anti-Terrorist system!' He strides behind the desk, presses a button under it. The partition retracts, silence reigns.

In the gardens, guards scramble, peer into hedges and behind fountains. 'Last place was blown up. We're safe as houses, behind that screen.' He marches over to

Her Majesty, opens a small door to Her right to reveal a miniature Sainsburys. 'We've enough food for a month.'

'Spiffing!' says Don.

Ashley shuffles from foot to foot.

'Take a pew.' Sir Rodney reclines on a black leather sofa. We huddle round the fax machine on British-designed chairs. Adjust the height of mine so my feet don't dangle. Ashley brings in a padded chair from Martha's ante-room for Don.

'Sir Ronald, I realise that you're very busy...' says Ashley sheepishly.

'Am I? How would *you* know that?' Ashley reddens.

'Your speech tonight gentlemen, will it be in Italian?'

Fuck.

'Not exactly...' We reply in unison.

Ashley turns to Don and me. 'There's the United Nations Food and Agriculture Organisation. They're entranced by our technological breakthrough...'

'Offices all over the globe will be able to communicate using the internet.'

'Into-what?' asks Sir Rodney, looking thoroughly confused.

'Internet.' I explain. Stunned silence.

Ashley continues, 'Then we've got three from ENI, the state oil business and... here's the list, forty in all.'

'Hmm, good job, Goodwin. 'Drink anyone?' Sir Rodney leads us to his drinks cabinet. Anything to change the subject...

Later that evening we stroll out of the meeting. 'They were eating out of our claws,' boasts Don, as we leave the Jolly Hotel into humid evening air. 'Mind you, I didn't like the way that guy from the Ministry of Energy put his fag out on your business card, Moses. We didn't make much of an impression there.'

'FAO and ENI were all over us. I reckon we can shift half-a-million of consultancy and software to those guys alone... What's Roland's problem? He obviously hates poor Ash.'

Don places his heavy arm round me, I wince. 'Ashley made a pass at Roland's wife. Nothing serious.' He lets go of me. We walk past *Via Veneto* piano bars. 'Both got pissed at the Embassy summer bash. Roland caught them snoggin' in the grotto. Roland's asked for a transfer to Singapore.'

'How do you know all this stuff, Don?... Don?'

Don's gone in a puff of smoke. Search sheepishly nearby bars. Scantily clad Latin hostesses proposition me. 'No, no, I'm looking for a friend, not sex.' Wander back to the Jolly Hotel, perplexed. Where's Don Smith, who lies about his birthday? Don Smith, former Lewisham washing-machine pleb salesman. Don Smith paid by the Mafia to shadow Commander Stern? Or screwing Vanessa?

6

The phone wakes me.

'Hello, Ricky? It's George.'

George? 'Oh, George! Where are you?'

I scan my strange hotel room: two double beds, uniform furnishings, matching pine wardrobe, chest of drawers, print of happy ice skaters.

'Hong Kong,' says George, 'how's Stockholm?'

I hate Stockholm, miserable, soulless pit. Pissed yobbos stumbling around the Old City.

'Freezing. Minus twenty.'

'And sales?'

'Nothing definite. We were mobbed in Rome. Also had interest from the Dutch and Belgians. The French useless. Information gathering. Off to the Embassy,' I glance at my bedside alarm, 'in one hour.'

'It's going a storm here,' says George. 'Meeting a Chinese Gov rep for dinner tonight to eat sheep's eyes.' George is on another planet.

'Listen Rick, we've had a call in from top knob in the German Government. Wants to meet tonight,' he continues.

'That's Don's patch.'

'Yeah, but Don's holed up in Monaco for the weekend,' says George.

'Plus, you know my Dad would be furious...'

'Mum's the word...' replies George not particularly reassuringly.

'And Don will be livid.'

'Look,' continues George. 'Just be at the Frankfurt Sheraton at 7pm. Meet Karl Schuler. Can you take on Mission Impossible?'

'Do my best.'

'Thanks, Rick. See you Monday at the office.'

Arghh!

Frankfurt Airport chaos, 30 mins to reach the Sheraton in the dark. Freezing, driving sleet. Taxi-less rank's a scrum. Eventually a cab arrives, vultures descend.

A timid couple stand to one side. Their secret weapon, a baby.

'You need a taxi?' I ask. 'If I get you one, can I have a lift to the Sheraton? It's only fifteen minutes from here.'

'For sure. But how will you get one?' The husband smiles nervously.

'Just follow me.'

We walk in the direction of oncoming taxis, swaying in buffeting winds. Drenched. The baby gasps and hiccups. The couple cower behind me. There's no going back.

In the distance, oncoming headlights.

As the taxi approaches, I jump into its path and hold out my hand. It skids to a halt. I pull open a back door.

'Quick! Get in!'

The couple hesitate, then pile onto the back seat. I follow.

The stunned driver passes the rank. Angry faces, gesticulating arms.

He clicks the automatic door lock. Edges forward through the mob and drives away.

'Tolle!' mutters the father.

I command, 'Sheraton Hotel, please. Then take these good people home.'

'You must be Karl Schuler.' He stands in front of Reception, tall, silver hair neatly in place. Sports a three-piece striped suit, silver fob watch, red handkerchief in top pocket.

'Their banks are awash with stolen Jewish money,' says Dad. 'Bloody Germans!'

'And you are Stein, Sir?' Strong Germanic twang.

'Richard Stern.'

He fumbles through a fax. *'Richtig!'* Pedantic, humourless arsehole.

We settle in a bar by a large window. The blizzard's subsided. Pretty snow-covered trees are lit by hotel searchlights. I'm wiped out by the exertions of the past week. I'll warm him up for Don, then catch the 9.30 p.m. flight home.

A stiff uniformed waiter serves orange juice to him, coffee to me. He sips through a straw.

'It is simple. Ve understand you usink new communications techniques for zis internet-thing. Ve vant conduct experiment. Ve fit two offices with your equipment and transfer data.

'And if it works?'

'Then ve buy software. Ve have ze price list.'

'Sounds fair. Our consultancy fee is...' Think of a number, any number, double it, add 50 grand, halve it, take away the number you first thought of, answer's, '25 thousand pounds.'

'Done, Stein. Let me pay for drinks, *bitte.*' He gestures to the waiter, who marches over.

'That's not necessary.' I reach for my wallet.

He tugs my arm. *'Nein, nein,* you my guest.' Blue eyes, cherubic face, commanding nose. 'I take you to airport on vay home.'

En route in a black BMW. 'What's that slogan?' I point at the rear mirror. *Die Nie-Aufgebenden.*

He sits stiffly, hairy hands outstretched. Driving a tank towards enemy lines. Surrender or die!

'What does it mean?'

'Never Give Up. I belong to a group. A religious order, for... how you says it?'

Madmen? 'Masons?'

'Nein, nein!' Manic laugh. Head jerks from side to side. 'For laymen. It's a code for laymen.'

'So, what do you believe?'

'Zat ze Vord of Man is ze Vord of God. Once commitment given, it must be followed through. No matter vhat hardships.' He glances at me.

Wish he'd keep his eyes on the road.

'He is of unsound Mind,' says God.

'You brought him into my life,' I reply.

'Reckless and impetuous! Your parents taught you nothing.'

'Ve also no smoke, drink or fornicate. Ve discourage business *mit zose* who do.' Don's sworn to give up smoking. 'Ricky, you model citizen, *ja*. Perhaps, you care to join us?'

'Yeah verily he is in the company of Idol Worshippers,' whispers God.

'I'm too weak-willed. What's the upside?'

'Upside?'

'Bonus.'

'A place at His right hand in ze Vorld to Come.'

Second prize? A trip to Valhalla?

'Here we are at airport. *Auf Wiederzehn,* Stein. Please, you fax me confirmation of order, *ja*. I look forward to our continued comradeship.'

'Thanks Karl, but your sales executive is Don Smith. He's abroad 'til Wednesday. I'll make sure he's in contact soon.'

'No, sorry, Stein. My order is personal to you. I have given my vord to you. My vord not transferable.'

No time to argue. 'Karl, we look forward to doing business with you.'

'Me, too.'

'Dreyfus!' says Don.

7

Our office is a war zone. Operation Zinger. Giant, plasticised charts are stuck to every wall. Today Italy, tomorrow the world! Don throws nicotine chewing gum, matches, keys and an expense claim onto his desk. He bungs gum in his mouth, lights up a Camel, dangles it from his mouth.

'Morning, Nixon,' he shouts.

'Shurely, some mishtake, Don,' I reply.

'Don't think so, Squire.'

'Nixon's not Jewish,' I protest.

'You don't say? Tell me something new. For example, why were you in Frankfurt Friday night?' Sweat stains under his jacket armpits.

'To see Schuler from the German Government.'

Vanessa arrives, dives for the Camel packet, takes Don's fag, lights up. 'Thought you said you could stop whenever you wanted to.' Says Don.

Smoke mingles with her sexy hair.

'Be a love, sweetheart, make me a strong coffee,' he commands.

'I'll have a tea, please,' I say politely.

Nil response from this tanned *prima donna* in mauve dress, sandals. She exits, nose in the air.

'So, Rasputin?' continues Don. Not Jewish either.

'Listen, George sent me. I told Schuler you'd be in touch today. What's the problem?'

'Take this, fucker!' He launches a fax dart at me, which lands on my desk.

I inspect the fax on German Government notepaper: *As discussed with Mr Stein, my order is personal to him. I look forward to hearing from him by return.*

'There was nothing I could do about it. Schuler's a member of a weird sect. *'Die Nie-Aufgebenden.* Once he promises something, he can't go back.' It sounds ridiculous.

'Beware, Ho Chi Ming, this is all out war!'

Don was a school bully: Gimme sixpence or I'll smash your fuckin' face in! And at the Lewisham Electricity Showroom: If you don't buy this washing machine, I'll bring my henchman to shut off your water supply!

Vanessa returns with a coffee for Don.

'Where's my tea?'

She draws on her fag and walks out. Urban warfare isn't my strong suit, especially when I'm up against Attila the Hun, and Lady Macbeth.

In the following days, our software staff program Karl Schuler's data for the experiment and install it. Everything works fine.

Karl's as good as his word. Everything you'd expect from a member of kinky *Die Nie-Aufgebenden.* Don's incensed. He storms into the office, slumps over his desk, sullenly writes sales proposals, disappears into the Boardroom to make secret calls.

I feel sorry for him. I offer to share commission, but he shrieks, 'Fuck off, Dreyfus! You're history.' A chill runs down my spine.

The Rome Embassy provides a tasty consultancy contract with FAO, and a major lead into the Italian Ministry of the Environment. I shuttle between Milan and Rome. I book tickets through Vanessa who knows my every move. I'm on a precipice.

Don plots my return to Fuse House but I can't fathom his tactics.

GRAPE Christmas Party at the Dorchester Club. Waiters hand out drinks at the door from silver trays. I've hired a Moss Bros dinner suit. Susie's stunning in a pleated crepe dress with a black top, ankle-length red skirt, black high-heels. We wait in line, holding champagne glasses.

Susie tugs my sleeve and whispers, 'Did you get the hoover fixed? The Cohens are coming over for dinner on Friday night.'

Behind us, George's wife, in a black sequined dress, prattles. 'We did get away last year, but *he* had to come back early.'

George, in starched white shirt, black dinner suit, gleaming black shoes, smiles at me and shrugs.

Lady and Sir Ramsey Duncan, GRAPE Chairman, greet us. 'I've heard all about your exploits, Ricky,' he says, 'ah, and this must be you charming wife?' Susie blushes. Why aren't I tall and debonair? Pleased to meet you Missus Ramsey, would you like to buy a software package? I'll git you a good discount.

'Can you pick up my folks from Gatwick tomorrow evening?' asks Susie.

Bloody hell. 'Of course, beautiful.'

We help ourselves to mini-canapés, served on small silver trays by out-of-work actors. 'Can't they afford real food?' asks Susie.

'Everyone here'll get pissed then leave for a late dinner.' Next year, I'll get Mum to make sarnies. Lady Ramsey, would you like a salt beef sandwich? Is it kosher? Oh yes, from Blooms. How very tantalisingly exotic!

Vanessa sprawls drunk in a corner. Tears stain her white silk evening dress with its low neckline. Her shoulder strap hangs loosely over her arm. Seccies huddle to comfort her. As she rises, her breasts spill out of her bodice. George's assistant, an attractive Mauritian in a green satin two-piece, tries to calm her.

Don approaches with frumpy wife in tow. 'Christmas greetings, old buddy, although I know you're not a Christian. Time for an armistice. May I introduce my wife, Gertrude?' About to shake Susie's hand, Don says, 'Saw you at the old *shiver.'*

Suddenly, a tearful Vanessa flies across the room, satin sandals undone, straps flying around her ankles. 'Excuse me...' She shoves Susie out of the way, slaps Don's face and storms out. Guests stare and mutter.

'Fuckin' cow! Bitch!' yells Don. I restrain him from chasing her.

He regains his composure. 'I forgot to give her a Christmas bonus.' Nervous titter. Stiff upper lip and all that. The party resumes as if nothing's happened.

George takes me to one side. 'Ricky, you don't think… Hmm, Van and Don?'

There were plenty of clues. 'If so, they're *finito!*' I reply.

'Quite.' George prods me, wanders back to Sir Ramsey.

'Don's a pig!' whispers Susie.

'At least Van will be making my tea again,' I reply.

The next morning, I mount the office stairs and catch Don rummaging through my card file, fag in mouth.

'Hey, what you up to?' I demand.

He continues flicking through card entries. 'Looking for Schuler's address, Rasputin.'

'For why?'

'If you got in at six, like what I do, you'd know.' He extracts a card, scribbles the address on his cigarette pack, returns to his desk. He chucks me a press release. 'Here, catch … Schuler's resigned.'

I brush ash off my desktop. 'For personal reasons?'

'Sorta nervous breakdown. Anyway, spoke to George. Germany's all mine again, so you can sod off! I'm meetin' Schuler's replacement. Since you're a loser, we might as well kiss and make up. No hard feelings, eh? Chop?' He holds out his hand.

I'm shaken. My heart pounds. That German deal was worth almost a million *spondulicks!* No commission and, more importantly, no prestige. I'll join the tramps in Lincoln's Inn Fields.

'I used to work in that building over there. I've still got my British Airways Executive Club card to prove it.' 'And I was Governor of the Bank of England,' boasts my fellow tramp. Don struts past railings, Vanessa on his arm. She says, 'Oh I'd absolutely adore going with you to St. Moritz, darling...'

At least, I've still got the Italian ENI contract.

Vanessa carries in two cups. 'Tea and coffee, boys?'

'Thanks, sweetheart. Fag?' Don proffers his pack.

'No, ta, got me own,' she smiles wanly. All lovey-dovey again.

I call Ashley in Rome. 'Hi, how's tricks?' Don leans sideways to eavesdrop.

'Heard you've sorted the legals out with ENI.'

'Yep, thanks to you. I'm coming over Thursday, for signature. Fancy dinner?' I ask.

'Sure, can we eat Chinese?'

Hate Chinese. 'But of course!' I reply.

Wednesday afternoon. I'm about to leave for Heathrow in a Crombie overcoat. The phone rings. I dump my overnight case on the carpet, lift receiver.

'That you, Shylock?'

'Don? Where are you?'

'In *Roma*. Don't you read your faxes? ENI wanted to sign today. You were a no-show, so I flew in from Zurich. Ash and I are off to celebrate. You're finished, buddy-boyo. Fuse House ain't so bad. For a loser, like yerself. By the by, Dad knows you don't have a C bloody E. *Ciao!*'

A lump rises in my throat. I shout, 'Vanessa!' and jump down the stairs.

She's embarrassed.

'Did a fax arrive for me?'

'Fax? Let's see, shall we?' She shuffles scraps of paper around. 'Here in your in-tray, didn't I tell you? Oh, I'm really sorry.' Hopeless liar.

It arrived last night from the Embassy to notify me that the meeting's this very afternoon! 'Bloody hell!'

I stomp down the corridor to George's office. He's in shirtsleeves completing The Times cryptic crossword. Dapper as always.

'Ricky, you look awful. What's up?'

I flop down in a guest chair, 'Don...'

'Ah, just put the phone down to 'im. What a superstar. And what a cock-up! You'll have to pull your socks up, young fellow. I'm promoting Don, with immediate effect. From now on, you report directly to him.'

I weigh up my options.

Scenario 1: Return to Electricity Commission, Fuse House. I'm assigned the lowest position: Lift boy. Pete says, 'I always knew you were a fraud.' Ted says, 'Jesus welcomes sinners.' Julie, Ted and Pete in unison, 'You've let us all down. Third floor please.'

Scenario 2: Stay at GRAPE. Don's lacky. 'Make Vanessa a coffee, Shylock. Light our fags.' I've no choice.

'George, I'm offering my resignation.'

He looks troubled, leans forward, says. 'You sure, Ricky? It's rather a harsh and hasty decision.'

I imagine myself as EC liftboy. 'Perhaps, George.'

'I understand, Ricky. An honourable move, if I say so myself.'

As we shake hands, he says, 'Pity you didn't join our Lodge.'

Maybe in my next non-kosher life.

I stuff belongings into my briefcase, head home.

'Fine mess you got me into! If it hadn't been for that CBE nonsense I'd be in Grade 2 Technical Development by now.'

'Trust in Me,' saith the Almighty. *'For my ways are Mysterious. No mere man can fathom the wisdom of the Lord!'*

As I walk into our road, I see Susie emerge from our car with a pile of exercise books. 'Thought you were in Rome, dear?' she says.

'I've news but it can wait.' I drop my bags and bend down to kiss her. 'Here, let me help you with those.' I clutch a pile of books, drop two on the floor. She stoops to pick them up.

'I've news too,' she says.

'You've gotta Jumble Sale in our garden this Saturday?' I guess.

'My period's late. I did one of the those tests this morning...'

'And...?' *Please, God, not.*

'I'm preggers!' she chirrups.

'Darling, that's wonderful news.' I hold her tightly.

Wet nappies in the bathroom, sleepless nights, breastfeeding, heating bottles. Post-natal depression, like her Mum? No job!

RING INN

8

What drew me to this Suffolk asylum? A few weeks ago, I luxuriated in the Jolly Hotel, Rome.

Susie urged me to come here to recharge my batteries. A week of meditation, while she *schmoozes* her Dad to hire me.

'What you going to do with the rest of your life, young man?' A fellow inmate addresses me.

'Work for myself. Become a serial entrepreneur.' I reply serving myself a second helping of spaghetti. Serial entrepreneur? Where did that come from?

'Guess...' says God.

'What?' She's in her seventies, bent, thin, stone deaf. She cups her hand behind her ear. A strand of veggie falls from her fork onto her plate. She places the empty fork in her mouth, looks puzzled.

I sprinkle sea salt over my food. 'Serial entrepreneur!' I say loudly.

I huddle with the others at a gigantic, pine table.

'Have you been to prison?' she croaks, edging her chair away.

'No, that's for criminals.' Come back Don, all is forgiven.

I hear the hoot of an owl, zoom of a passing car. Consider a walk across the mown lawns to stargaze under plane trees and oaks. Maybe find a local piano bar!

'I might have something for you,' says Hamish. He's in his fifties, clear blue eyes, curly ginger hair, narrow face, black-rimmed specs, tanned clear skin.

'Tell me.'

He cuts his spaghetti into bite-sized pieces. 'Something I was working on at Telecom, before I retired.' Energy-saving bulbs flicker as he chomps away.

'Really?' I'm intrigued.

He chews, swallows. 'Yep. Telephone Information Services. Speaking Clock, Weather, Racing…'

'Over the phone?' I ask.

'Exactly.' He pushes his plate aside, stretches over, takes a mug, emblazoned *Southwold,* wanders over to the hot water urn. He spoons Barley Cup, adds hot water.

Another fellow leans forward, elbow on the table. 'Surely, nobody rings the Speaking Clock?'

'Only 250 million people a year. At 10 pence each, actually,' replies smug Hamish. He leans against the doorframe, sipping his health drink.

'Really? I'm impressed. That's 25 million quid. What about other services?' I ask.

'450 million calls a year in total. Whole set up forced to close. Government orders. Being replaced by private operators. Would you, Ricky, care to be one?'

Ricky Stern. Mr Telephone. Has a certain ring to it.

'How?'

'When you get back, contact my replacement, Matt Grabball. He'll fill you in.'

'You smuggle a bird in last night?' asks Hamish on my last morning.

We're alone drinking coffee. I see others strolling round the grounds deep breathing before breakfast. A grey squirrel darts along the oaks.

'I should be so lucky.'

'Thought I heard you moan.' He shifts back and forth on his chair, hands under thighs.

I recall the night's excitement: bedtime, warm milk and honey, hot water bottle, freezing room. 'Oh, I had a weird dream...'

He grins, taps my arm. 'Sounded like you were in ecstasy. Tell me about it. I studied Dream Therapy at Esalen.'

I gaze at a watercolour of a mountain and recall my dream. 'I'm at the offices of *Everard and Dyar.'*

'Dry cleaners?'

'City law firm. Deal closure going on. Three fat businessmen and me are passing round papers to sign...' Hamish nods wisely.

'Now for the real business,' I say in the dream. I extract my napkin from a gold ring, place the ring in the centre of the table. The fat businessmen turn into marzipan men. I gobble them up. Delicious!'

'It's quite clear,' says Hamish. 'Three fatties are competitors. After three years, you'll eat 'em alive. And the significance of the gold ring?'

Circle? Marriage? 'Got it! Ring... telephone... geddit?'

'Can't say I do.' Hamish's quizzical bushy grey eyebrows arch.

'Your telephone info idea...!' I yell.

'So, you'll get rich from that phone business.' Hamish smiles.

God has spoken. I shall do as He commands. Why can't He speak in plain English? Thanks to Hamish's dream training, I won't be working for Dad-in-law, selling Persian carpets.

I hastily load my suitcase into nifty secondhand green Nissan Micra, bought with my GRAPE severance pay. Can't deal with the real world of telephone services and a pregnant wife, just yet.

I hurtle through narrow Suffolk lanes singing my own version of "Born To Be Wild" at the top of my voice to startled villagers—

'Get the Micra running/Head out on the A12/Looking for a teashop... /What a lovely taste/Born to drink tea-eee/Born to drink tea-eee.'

I mark each teashop. Does it have China crockery, silver cutlery, waitresses in pinafores? I breakfast in Teapots and Quails, in Framlingham. I order full English Tea, with toasted teacakes, scones and clotted cream, then drive slowly towards West Hampstead.

Our hall's been re-carpeted in revolting dark mauve. I find Susie in the kitchen, who asks, 'Did you wipe your feet? Daddy thought we'd like a new carpet to celebrate my preggers.' The smell of cooking makes me bilious.

She glances my way, stirs a pan with her right hand. 'He's happy to employ you as an Area Sales Executive.'

I lay my hands on her shoulders, watch a Dunlop air balloon floating in the distance, nuzzle her neck. She's barefoot. Her blue-striped apron covers her thick, red woollen jumper.

'Someone gave me a business idea,' I begin.

'You'd accompany one of the reps, 'til you'd learnt the ropes. Then he'd fire them.' She continues oblivious.

Couscous in the saucepan. I lied on our first date, said I loved them. Now we have them every ruddy meal. 'I don't want to work in carpets...'

'Father would be so pleased. The business has been in the family for generations.'

I clutch my stomach, 'Something I ate for breakfast...'

'Poor you! Will you consider it?' I head towards the loo and throw up. I knew I should have stopped at four scones.

'You sure Mr Grabball knows I'm waiting?'

'Yeah,' sniffs the haughty Telecom receptionist. 'He's still in his meeting, won't be a tic.' She arranges the message pad, pens, calendar and black plastic Telecom clock on her desk.

I return to the plush Reception area in the atrium of Endeavour Tower. Glass-sided lifts glide up and down carrying self-important executives in uniform grey suits. They stand like erect dummies clutching files and folders.

Reception has neat copies of the *Financial Times* on tables and two castrated palm trees. A city oasis. I pace up and down. Outside the window, freezing city workers rush by. I find the Telecom Annual Report in a book rack. One billion pounds profit, yet they can't make my meeting on time!

Half-an-hour later, 'Mr Stern? Mr Grabball will see you now. Follow me?' She's a young brunette in a black power mini-skirt. The lift has a see-through floor. Arghh, vertigo! Spiderstern backs into a corner, gropes glass behind his back, suctions himself to it.

'You can see the whole City from here,' squeaks the brunette. Buildings and windows reel below me.

'Lovely,' I reply. Half-shut eyes reveal she's ogling a stripped window cleaner in jeans, held close to the wall by a fragile cradle.

'He must be freezing.' She waves to him. He waves back, wolf whistles.

I stumble out of the lift, trip against a wall, regain my balance, chase after her. 'This is Mr Grabball's office. Take a seat.'

Functional grey, regulation seat, steel desk. I sit with my back to the window and read Telecom promotional posters – 'You're never alone with a phone.' Heard that before.

A weasel appears. Thirties, blond, round spectacles, shifty. Unregulatory brown suit. No tie! A subversive?

Grabball looks through me, slumps into a seat, asks, 'What can I do for you?' No apology, no handshake, no tea, no eye contact. Fiddles with a paperclip, gazes out the window at the stray window cleaner.

'Hamish McDonald told me...' I relax my body, rest my hands on my knees, uncross my legs and keep them slightly apart.

He stiffens. '*You* know McDonald?'

Hamish has retired. He's no threat, Stoatface. I play innocent. 'I met him on a retreat.'

He looks at me for the first time. Sneers, 'A retreat?'

Perhaps business-like is required? 'He told me you had to privatise your information services.'

'What concern's that of yours?' Grabball scowls.

'I'm considering becoming a private operator.'

'With respect...' He gives me the once over, '*Who* are you? I've never heard of you.'

Ricky Stern. Ex-CBE. Adventurer and failed computer software salesman. 'I'm...'

I hear a tap. The window cleaner points at his empty wrist, mouths, 'Time?' I thrust my arm towards him so he can read my watch. Avoid looking down into the street.

Grabball says, 'Let me offer you some free advice. You're wasting your time.'

'Why?'

'We're only granting licences to reputable companies. Companies of substance, not one-man bands.'

'How do you know I'm...'

He points at me. 'Are you a company? What's its capitalisation? Three-year trading? Need I continue?'

'I get the picture.'

'Goodbye, Mr Stern.' He points to the door. 'Lift's to the right.' He opens a file, starts scribbling. I notice a stack of photocopies on a cabinet behind him, entitled *Information Service Statistics.*

'May I have one of those photocopies, please?'

'Why not?' Without looking up, he reaches behind him, grabs a booklet, slides it across his desk, mutters, 'You can use it as toilet paper.'

At home, on the sofa with Susie beside me. I open a school report, hand it to her, wait for her to write comments.

Hamish rings on our cordless phone.

Get anywhere with Grabball?' He asks.

'I got humiliated and vertigo. Prince Charming will only deal with so-called reputable companies, not scumbags like me.'

Susie stops writing, pokes me, mouths, 'Talk to Daddy!'

'I wouldn't exactly call you a scumbag!' laughs Hamish.

'Anyway, it's a non-starter,' I reply.

I circuit the room, phone to my left ear. Straighten the nude Modigliani print by the door, scan paperbacks, prayer books, encyclopedias in a handmade bookcase. 'What services will you run? They must consider a good plan,' says Hamish.

God knows.

'Do I?' he replies.

I open *Information Service Statistics* on our glass coffee table, search for relevant data. 'The most popular are Racing and Horoscopes. I'm not clued up on either.'

Hamish advises me to contact racing correspondent, Terry Tomblin and Universe astrologer, Cosmic Benny. 'Not that I believe that tosh,' he declares.

I grab Susie's pen to make notes on *The Guardian.*

When the call is over, Susie says, 'Darling… '

'Yes, dear?'

'You'd make a good living.'

'Selling crummy magic carpets?'

Her freckled brow frowns, 'It's better than this unreliable Telecom nonsense.'

I'd rather roast in hell.

'Such could be thy Fate,' says an unforgiving God.

9

I start the hunt for a portfolio of phone services. First stop, Terry Tomblin. Well known BBC horse racing journalist. I wrote him a letter and to my surprise, he rang me back.

'You're a fuckin' genius!' shouts Terry.

'That's very kind of you, Terry.' My sort of bloke, one who appreciates me.

We arrange to meet for afternoon tea the next day at Brown's Hotel, seated by a fire in a corner nook. Mini-salmon sarnies, Madeira cake, scones, cream, jam, tea.

'Bloody fuckin' genius!' He's very Irish, mischievous, magical. Lightweight fawn sports jacket and flannels.

He eyes a pretty waitress. 'So, you'll be giving racing results and tips on the phone?'

'Correct.'

'And you'll make dosh every time someone calls?'

My plush, red settee's so deep, I struggle to sit upright. 'That's right, Terry.'

'We'll make a fortune!' We? The leprechaun bounces up and down. His thinning white hair has a pinkish scalp tint.

'Providing they call. Where shall I advertise numbers?' I ask.

'You don't wanna advertise, matey.'

'Can I be getting you something?' The waitress's freckled, baby face beams into Terry's leer. Blond, curly hair falls onto her shoulders.

'You wouldn't be from Ireland like, would yer, me darlin'?' asks Terry.

She flushes. 'Cork.'

'Oh, so yer a Cork lassie, are yer?' He chats her up, relentless. A pianist bashes out Strangers In the Night. She totters off under Terry's lecherous stare.

'You were saying?' he asks.

'You were explaining why we don't have to advertise.'

He slurps his tea, adds a mound of sugar, guzzles. 'Jesus! For a genius, you're right fuckin' stupid...' Charming. 'We'll do a deal with Racing On. They'll promote numbers and we'll split profits with 'em.'

'Will they do a deal?' I lift a mini-strawberry pastry with a silver fork from a silver cake dish.

'Course they bloody will. It's money for nowt. Anyway, Graham...'

'Graham?'

'The editor... Graham fuckin' Tucker's like a brother.'

'Fucker Tucker's, Terry's brother.' I rhyme.

He shakes the armrest of my settee. 'You're fuckin' crazy! When can we start? I need a few weeks to get a team of journos together.'

'Journos? I only need one guy,' I reply.

'One guy? One guy? How many fuckin' race meetings d'yer think there are this comin' Bank Holiday Monday? I'll tell you, matey—sixteen. One guy? This is gonna be a *professional* operation, Boyo.'

The next port of call is with The Universe paper's well-known astrologer.

Cosmic Benny, alias Benjamin Kovitz, lives in a bedsit off Archway Road. The terraced house is derelict. Peeling painted front door, cracked windowpanes, wonky drainpipes. I press the rainbow motif bell marked "Benny" in red. Slowly, Jesus in a kaftan answers the door. Greasy, shoulder-length hair, dirty feet in bare sandals.

'You followin' me, man?' Nasal drone through the half-open front door.

'I'm Ricky Stern. I phoned earlier.' Paranoid?

'Welcome, man.'

He leads me up four gloomy flights, to a squalid room. The smell of damp, incense, hash, rotting food. Unmade bed, greasy cooker in a corner, knee-high table with Indian floor cushions. "Tubular Bells" on his stereo.

'Earl Grey?' He shuffles to the cooker, lights the gas ring with a shaky hand. I've made a tragic mistake.

'You *are* Cosmic Benny?'

'How can you ask that, man? My mug's in two-million papers every day. Bet you've never even read Universe.'

I stare at the spider's web on the ceiling, 'I expected a famous astrologer, like yourself, to be living... well, differently...'

I squat on a limp cushion. He sits opposite me. 'They're all a rotten bunch of thieves and liars!' He vigorously stirs the brew inside a chipped brown teapot with an HB pencil.

'Those buggers at Universe. You're not like them.' He pours weak tea into mugs with dirty brown stains, 'You're honest, I can sense that. Good Karma.'

'Ta, Ben.' At last, someone thinks I'm honest. Shame it has to be this retard, soaked in mystic claptrap.

His mood switches, 'What d'yer want, man?' The hint of aggression. 'I need bread to support my lifestyle. Will you gimme dough, man?' His eyes glint, his body tilts alarmingly to the right.

'Er, yeah. I'll need you to record horoscopes every week from our offices. Not exactly sure when...'

He places his forefinger on my lips. 'Cool. No details now, man. Buzz me.'

'Don't you want to know the deal?' I wipe my mouth with a tissue.

His pupils dilate. 'Nah, like I said, I trust you, just gimme cash. Now if you don't mind, I'm expectin' a friend.'

I leave my mug untouched, follow him down creaky stairs. He clutches a wooden bannister for support and nearly misses his step.

The brown stair carpet encrusted with mud looks vaguely familiar. 'May I ask where you bought this carpet?'

'You want to buy it, man.'

'No, it just reminds me of one in my house.'

Benny's thinking, 'Outside Sam's Carpet store in the Archway Road in a skip.'

'My father-in-law's shop! What a small world.

He wipes his finger on his kaftan, says, 'You'd better believe it, man.'

My accountant, Mel Silver, rolls up his blue shirt sleeves and peers at a spreadsheet. 'Let me get this right. They call you, you get cash. That doesn't seem right?'

His veneered desk is stacked with family photos, diplomas, and prints of The Wailing Wall, Safed and Masada hang on cream walls.

'They don't actually call me, they call my computer.'

'For racing results,' he taps keyboard. 'Horoscopes,' tap. 'Quizzes,' tap. 'What else?' Mouth puckers, eyes half-closed.

'Not sure yet. Let's add two miscellaneous services?' tap-tap.

'Cost of call?'

'50p per minute,' tap.

'Length?'

'Say, 90 seconds?'

He relaxes, stretches out his legs, raises arms behind his head. 'Did I tell you I was the first accountant in the West End to use Excel?'

'Yes, several times...' I try not to sound annoyed.

'Telecom share?'

'50%.'

'Number of calls?'

'1,000 per day, for each service,' tap.

'And your computer can handle more than one call at a time, right?'

'Yep, up to 30.'

'Will calls come in uniformly throughout the day?'

'40% will come within 30 mins of the end of each race. Let's assume 90% of the rest before 9 p.m.'

'That leaves a few calls overnight.' Mel continues tapping.

'Fine,' I reply.

Tap-tap-tap.

'Shame you got married.' The printer churns out figures.

'Why?'

'You're gonna be a rich man. I'd introduce you to my daughter.' I glance at his family portraits. She's probably the smaller girl wedged between Mel and Mrs Silver. I'd roll in the hay with her any day. 'She needs a *mensch* like you. 'Stead of that *schlemiel* she's dating.'

He tears off the printer paper and lays it on the desk between us. 'Look, it's unbelievable. I've doubled the cost of your computer hardware and labour and halved your call projections. First-year sales are still over 2 million quid; profit's around half-a-mill.'

If I were a rich man... 'But they're only projections. How much cash will I need to raise?'

'Let me look at the cash flow.' He flicks through the printout, using a plastic letter opener as a guide. 'You'll need £300k to be safe. You go cash positive in month 5, then you milk it.'

'But where am I going to get that sort of dough? I'm eating through my savings from GRAPE as it is. Can't even afford a Chinese takeaway.'

'Go to *Keifeng.* Mention my name, they'll give you 10% off.' He's suggesting his fave Chinese gaff.

'Be serious.'

He lays down the printout. 'I'll fix for you to meet Dan Sharpstone at Irony. You'll hit it off with him. Bit of a go-getter.'

'Irony?'

'It's what we call a venture capital company. They raise money from rich bastards and Dan "invests" it. They have so much spare dosh, they don't know what to do with it! But you'll need a name for your new cash cow.'

'Moo?' I jest.

'Ha, ha!'

'Ring-Inn. The Home of Telephone Information.' I try again.

'You're joking.' Mel's mouth opens.

'It's tacky, memorable. Like me,' I reply.

'Done. I'll set it up. Ring-Inn Ltd it is!'

Next day at Dan Sharpstone's office, he pulsates into the room. Vroom! 'Sorry to keep you waiting.' All of thirty seconds. 'I'm swamped by memos...'

'You've gotta great set-up here!' I comment. It resembles the sitting room of a private residence. Bright airy room overlooking Marylebone High Street.

Terry, Dan and I sit in armchairs around a low coffee table.

'It's a spare home of one of our investors, Ronny Handforth.' explains Dan.

'That's the geezer above the fireplace.' Terry points to a formal portrait of a Ball-bearing Magnate. His lined face looks benevolently down at us.

'You knew Ronny Handforth? I'm impressed,' says Dan.

Terry's bullshitting again.

'Sure, Ronny and I went to the same school. 'Course he was much older than me. Spoke at a school reunion a few years before he died. We became close friends.'

I can't keep *schtumm* and chip in. 'But, I've read about Ronny. He grew up in Leeds. You're from...'

'Dublin. Ronny's folks sent him to board at St. Ignatius. That's where he got his interest in ball-bearings. He was involved in a collision. Bike a write-off but all these ball-bearings were scattered over the road... he saw his whole future in a nutshell. The rest is history.'

'Fascinating.' Dan's fallen for this cobblers. The money's as good as in the bank. 'Now, about your plan. We hate it.' Dan stares at me.

'Then why are we here?'

'We hate it, 'cos it's too good.' He laughs and looks at Terry for feedback. Terry's quivering with laughter. This must be Venture Capital Humour.

'Really?' Shall I laugh or cry?

'Yes, really. You've done a deal with Racing On and Universe's Astrology page?'

'They're salivating. Can't wait to get going?' interrupts Terry, over-egging as usual.

'And that Astrologer chap?' continues Dan. A grandfather clock bongs three.

'Cosmic Benny?' I ask.

'Yeah, him, he's onside?' asks Dan.

'Totally.'

'Hmm!' Dan skims through the plan, glances at us. Glossy, brown hair flops over his brow. He flicks it back with his right hand. 'I'm minded to recommend this to our investment committee. We'll give you £300k. £150k for 30%, plus £150k as an unsecured loan. Howzat?'

Brilliantissimo. 'I could live with that.'

'We'll need you to invest £50k yourself, Ricky. To retain your 70%. Fancy investing, Mr Tomblin?'

Terry blanches. 'I'll stick to racehorses,' he titters.

Dan jumps up. 'Ok, gentlemen, I'll get back to you within 48 hours.'

We glide downstairs along to Maison Sagne in the High Street, sit beside a gold-framed wall mirror. *Émigrés* talk foreign on adjoining tables. A uniformed waiter delicately serves us English Breakfast Tea and éclairs.

'What was all that crap about, Terry?' I attack my éclair, cream spurts from my lips, I wipe them with the back of my hand.

'What kinda crap would that be?' he asks indignantly. He places his hands on his armrests and glowers.

'The crap about you knowing Ronny Handforth?'

'Your point is?'

I feel crass. 'What if Dan checks?'

Terry extracts a scrapbook from his black leather briefcase. It's stuffed with photographs and press cuttings. He turns pages, stops, says, 'Aha!' and hands a photo to me. 'Remind you of anyone?' I peer at a group of students, which includes Terry with Ronny Handforth. 'That's St. Ignatius.' He points to a Gothic building in the background. He snaps the book shut, returns it to his briefcase. 'So, what do you say, Rick?'

'I'm sorry I doubted you Terry.' He chuckles, forks a chocolate pastry into his mouth with a small silver fork.

The proprietor, Stanley, pokes his head over the cabinet of cream cakes, recognises Terry and says, 'Good to see you, Mr T. And how are we today?'

'Wonderful Stanley. How's the Missus?'

'We're all well. I'm retiring in a few months, you know?'

'That so? This is my crazy colleague, Ricky.' Stanley waves, then turns to a customer waiting to pay.

'Ain't there no-one you don't know, Terry boy?' I ask.

'Heh-heh-heh!' His craggy faces trembles with delight.

'Now tell me, Tel, where am I gonna find 50 bloody k?'

'Ring your accountant buddy, what's his name... Gold?'

'Silver.'

Shortly after, at home, there's a knock at our door. It's Mel Silver on his way home.

'Come in, come in! Excuse the chaos.' I wave him indoors.

'Renovating, eh?' He stares at our old bath, which stands on a white sheet in the hallway. We hired an Irish builder who gutted the bathroom but hasn't been seen since.

I hang Mel's coat and scarf on our wooden coat stand and escort him through debris to our living room. He wears red braces under an expensive blue suit, matching striped tie, large collar white shirt.

He extracts an A4 pad from his thin leather briefcase, a green folder marked "Stern" with a steel propelling pencil, leafs through the folder.

'Look,' says Mel, 'I'll get straight to the point. I can get you a mortgage which would free up 50k for you to take up the Irony deal, but I must advise you not to take it.'

'So why are you suggesting it?!'

'Because you don't have much choice! You've no trading record, no savings and your only asset is this place.' He circles his arm around signifying our flat.

'How much is this flat worth?' He inspects the room.

'We paid £200,000. It's probably worth £250,000 now. I've currently got a £150k mortgage.'

He makes a brief entry, says, 'And your salary will be in the Irony deal?'

'It'll be £60k, once Irony funds are in place.'

Mel continues, 'The mortgage company would give you a £230k mortgage based on the value of your Ring-Inn shares. They'd set repayments at a comfortable level. But if interest rates go up, and they surely will, you'll still pay the same each month but the additional interest will be added to the money you owe them. They'd also need a personal guarantee secured on this flat... and your shares.'

I nod. 'I understand.'

What's he talking about?

'Are you really sure, Ricky? I can only suggest you investigate an alternative source of funding.'

I've sorted out my 50k Irony investment, but I have a queasy sinking feeling in the pit of my stomach.

10

Sonny Fiori, President of Global Publications, places a foot on his black walnut desk, asks warmly, *'Come stai!* What d'ya think of these shoes?' He's a tall, thin, Italian Prince. Long face, hooded eyes, Roman nose. 'Got 'em at Grand Central this morning.' He says pointing at his shoes.

I squirm in my red and green striped tub chair. 'Well they're... unusual.'

He caresses his tie. *'E Questo?'*

Symmetrical dizzy red, white and blue cubes. 'Very snazzy.'

He admires his reflection in the windowpane, straightens sleek grey jacket, approaches me. He pinches my linen sleeve with suntanned fingers, purrs, *'Che carina stoffa.'* I took a decision a few weeks back to smarten myself up. Seems to have paid off!

'Thanks.... Liberty's. They do their own designer range.'

He rearranges family 'photos, pulls a silver chain and switches on a green-shaded Art-Deco table lamp.

'Liberty's... Nice name... Freedom!'

'Indeed...'

He beams, 'We'd like to have a presence in *Inghilterra*. We've an *amico* there now who feels we need a local partner; someone we can trust. We do lotto, gee-gees, 'scopes, everythin', 'cept porn. Luigi, out there...' He exchanges waves with a short guy tearing across the office. 'Luigi'd do porn. Always says, 'Sonny, why don't we try a little titillation?' but I say, 'Luigi, what ya talkin' 'bout? We're a *family* business. We don't need that sort of 'ting. *E chiaro?'*

He stops speaking and stares at me.

God says, 'He is not of Our Faith.'

'Your point?'

'For him, the body is Fornication.'

I wait for a police siren to quieten on Third Avenue twenty storeys below. 'Oh, absolutely, I shan't touch porn with a barge pole either...'

'Barge pole?' Sonny throws me a quizzical look.

'Slang,' I explain.

'So, what brings yer to New York?' continues Sonny.

I look directly at him. 'I've an offer from a bank to set up a premium calls business in London. I'm researching the States market for comparables.'

His face lights up. 'So, you wanna see *our* figures?'

'You'd agree to give me them?'

He claps. 'Sure, why not?' Because I'm a complete stranger?

He strides across parquet floor to a glass door, past a closed mahogany drinks cabinet with lattice outlay, empty ice-bucket in its recess and hollers, 'Luigi, gotta minute? Come in 'ere. Lika you to meet Ricky Stern. He's settin' up an operation like ours in *Inghilterra.'*

I stroll over to join them by the open door and shake Luigi's hand.

Luigi's squat and sturdy. Probably got his flat pug face from a fight. Short-sleeved, open-necked white shirt, brown trousers, matching leather slip-ons. 'That so? Pleased to make your acquaintance.' Firm handshake.

'Luigi, can you give Mister Stern here the doc you prepared for our shareholders?'

'The one with all the stats?' confirms Luigi.

I catch Sonny's wink. It's one big act and I'm the fall guy.

'Sure, that same one. Stern needs data to help him raise funds.'

Luigi's fingers rustle imaginary money. 'Funds? We've got funds.'

Sonny thumps Luigi's shoulder. 'Luigi! Great idea!'

Luigi staggers and I catch his arm. Sonny turns to me, 'You need dough, Stern, we got dough. Have you done the deal yet? How much they puttin' up?'

Why do I suspect he already knows? '£300k for 30%,' I reply.

Luigi and Sonny stare at each other and shrug.

'We'll match that,' says Sonny. He crosses his arms. Luigi holds my elbow. 'We like you, Stern.'

'For straight equity? No loan element?' I ask.

'D'Accordo,' agrees Luigi.

God interjects: *'Do not betray Irony.'*

'Gentlemen, that's extremely kind of you, but the deal's virtually done. You guys would take time.'

Sonny and Luigi wilt like jilted lovers. 'You could have the money by three this afternoon,' Sonny teases.

'That really is very kind, but I must stick with Ironico.'

'Irony?' asks Luigi.

'It's the name of my British bank.'

Luigi and Sonny clutch their stomachs and laugh.

Sonny gasps, 'Excuse us. Luigi, you better get Stern those figures.' Luigi lurches off. 'Hey Luigi?'

'What, Sonny?'

'Do yer lika my shoes?' Sonny stands on one leg, clasps the doorframe and kicks out his right foot, toe down.

Luigi strokes the leather shoe, looks up deferentially. 'Sonny, they're terrific! *Fantastico!*'

Matt Grabball makes a poor attempt at eye contact. He almost shakes my hand, but thinks better of it. I lower my dangling hand, sit opposite him. He's only kept me waiting ten minutes.

I begin, 'I'll get right to the point. I'm very excited by the premium calls business. I've got a plan, projections, backing from Irony...'

'What's Irony?' He doodles on a yellow post-it pad.

'A large venture capital fund. I've included their annual report in this pack. Also, joint venture agreements with Racing On and Universe.' His head jerks.

He stops scribbling, distracted 'Universe?'

'The Astrology column but it's a start. I'd really like a general contract.'

I try not to fidget. Finally, he says, 'Let me see what I can do for you. Can you leave those with me?' He gestures at the papers on my knees.

I hand over the documents and he skims through them.

'So when will you know?' I ask.

He smiles weakly. 'It's Friday today. We'll get back to you next week.' He shakes my hand limply and I leave, counting my fingers.

I'm practising "House of the Rising Sun" on my guitar. Nobody can murder it like me. The phone rings, I place the guitar in its black metal stand and run to pick up the cordless. A chirpy voice says, 'Mr Stern? Hello, I'm Stewart Day from Telecom. Matt Grabball's replacement.'

'Replacement?' I smell a rat.

'Yes, he left Friday. Didn't he tell you? Going private, setting up a premium calls business.'

'What?' I recall the sinking feeling I had at GRAPE as I pace up and down my living room.

'I understand you're also keen to set one up too.'

'Correct.' I examine an unopened bottle of Johnny Walker and a magnum of Bollinger in gift wrapping wedged in between *World Atlas* and old *National Geographics* in my bookcase.

'Do you have details? A plan would be helpful.'

The penny drops. 'I gave Grabball all my plans!' Opening the whisky, I read the label to calm my nerves.

'I'm sorry, Matt left in rather a hurry. We can't locate your file.'

Grabball! That weasel-faced, duplicitous, thieving bastard! The lying toe rag's stolen all my plans! Exterminate, exterminate.

I breathe deeply. 'Don't worry, I'll bike you a duplicate set.' Grabball's lower than a worm, as Mum would say.

'Would you mind? Only we want to encourage as many companies as possible.'

'You're not vetting?' Another Grabball lie!

'No, not really. Who told you that? That's not for Telecom. An independent body's being organised to monitor individual companies and services.'

I've been robbed.

Don's voice echoes, 'You're finished, Einstein.' And Pete's, 'Clear off scabbie!'

Not this time. Stern fights back. Commander Stern at the helm.

Neville Barclay, my solicitor, is the sanest member of our extended family. Handsome, early sixties, balding silver hair, baby-bum smooth chin.

'Now, somewhere... ah, got it!' He raises a large, black ring binder from the floor, deposits it on his antique teak desk below an IKEA table lamp. 'The documents from Irony. Everything will be ready for signature by the weekend.'

An eerie ringing comes from under the pile. He looks baffled, pats the pockets of his navy handmade suit. Lifts files, an antique carriage clock, Buddha, to find an old Bakelite phone. He lifts the handset to his ear. 'Yes, he's here. Put him through.'

He looks my way, 'For you. Dan Sharpstone from Irony. Apparently, it's urgent.' He struggles with the black phone cable to free it from a pile of unread clients' letters and hands me the receiver.

'Sorry to disturb you, Ricky, but I've news you won't appreciate,' says Dan.

'You're backing out?' My stomach wobbles. Neville's eyes commiserate. He shuts the file, searches his desk for a small notepad.

Dan continues. 'Course not. It's, well... a guy named Grabball popped in last week... saw one of my colleagues... impressed him... and, well, it seems Irony's backing him too.'

I shout, 'That lying bastard stole my plans and probably those of all my competitors!'

'Frankly, that's what makes the deal so attractive.' Dan makes light of it.

I open my mouth wide, stretch out my arms. The phone cable knocks over the table lamp. A perplexed Neville rights the lamp. I count to ten, stand and thrust the receiver to my mouth, 'Don't you lot have any bloody scruples?'

'We're bankers. But fear not, we've Chinese Walls. Absolutely no information about your business will get back.' Oh, yeah?

'Anyhow, thought it best I broke the news personally. Everything'll be fine. See you Friday at the closing meeting.'

I hand Neville the receiver and pace around his small office. There's no room between his desk, bookcase of arcane law and small black leather armchair.

'Grabball, my initial contact at Telecom has abandoned ship, run off with my confidential business plans and is setting up in competition. And Irony is backing him! What d'yer think of that!'

Neville places his arms his behind head. 'D'yer have an alternative?'

I remember Sonny and Luigi, You want dough? We got dough. 'Maybe. May I use your phone to call the States?'

Neville uses both hands to place an ancient telephone on the corner of his desk. 'Be my guest.'

I extract my Filofax from my briefcase and search amongst jottings for Sonny's direct line. The old phone taps out a connection to the New World. A single ring and Sonny's on the line.

'Sonny, I've changed my mind. Will you still back me?'

'Stern, we know we can do business with you. Fax me your account details and we'll wire you cash. £300k, right? Let's make it 500k, ok?'

'I'll fax you details, but what about the legal work? I'm with my lawyer.' Neville looks up from the file, lowers his hands, mouths, 'Slow down.'

Sonny says, 'Trust us Stern, we're men of honour.'

'I'll fax you my account details but, do me a favour, and wait 'til you see draft contracts.' Neville gives thumbs up.

'Whatever you want. We understand. We're relaxed about it.'

'I'd better do a search, Ricky. What's 'e called?' asks Neville.

'Sonny Fiori.'

'Don't do anything 'til I've checked 'im out,' he commands.

The next day, breakfasting at Maison Sagne, my new mobile warbles. I press a button, hold it to my ear. 'It's Nev, you'd better get over here.'

'I'll be 30 mins. I'm finishing breakfast.' I'm not rushing my cappuccino. He's probably found a double negative in the Irony contract. I pay my bill, then wander round to his office.

'Please sit,' he says.

He lifts a computer printout. 'All this is the dirt on your so-called ally Sonny Fiori. Take a look.'

He's highlighted words like: manslaughter, larceny, fraud, pornography, acquitted.

'Crikey!' I say.

'Lucky escape, no?' says Neville. He closes the printout, stuffs it into my folder, drops the folder on the floor.

'Hope so,' I reply, wanly.

'You *hope* so? What the hell do you mean?' he leans forward, eyes and nostrils narrow.

'Well, I did fax him company bank details,' I confess.

'You did *what?* I *warned* you not to do anything! You must check your account balance immediately.'

'But...'

Neville sighs. 'Check it now, Ricky!'

Sonny and Luigi stuff me into a body bag, toss me over Brooklyn Bridge into East River. I float to the bot-

tom, free myself and gaze into Don Smith's face. 'Game's over,' he shrieks. 'Loser!'

I call my bank. They confirm that $500k has been deposited in my account. On Nev's orders, I instruct them to return the money to the originator, Sonny Fiori.

'Ricky, Ricky, Ricky!' says Neville, shaking my shoulders from behind. 'Now, call your States-side friend and tell *him*.'

I'm panic-stricken.

I wait an age for the phone to connect. 'Sonny? Hi, it's Ricky.'

'Ricky! *Come stai?* Fog in *Londra?*'

Neville cranes to listen, scrawls on a pad, mutters, 'Get bloody on with it!'

'Sonny, I'm afraid I've made a mistake. It was too late to back out of the Irony deal. I'm going to have to go with them, after all.'

The line crackles, *'Un errore, Stern?* We had a deal. We wire the money.' Probably already ordering the body bag. Medium height, 10 stone.

'I've wired it back t-to y-you,' I stutter.

'Wired it back? You crazy? We had a fuckin' deal!' Don't be cross with me or I'll disintegrate. 'We're men of honour, you know that?' So, I see from that printout character assassination.

'I'm *really* sorry to have messed you about.'

'Stern, *momenta,* you hold.'

'Sure, Sonny.' Ordering the body-bag. A hired hitman?

Neville and I sit in silence. He chews his biro, I twiddle my thumbs.

Eventually, Sonny speaks, 'Stern, there's some shopping I must do in *Londra domani.* I plan to buy a linen suit like yours, at Liberty's. Meet me in Suits at 5 p.m. Okay?' Click.

'Liberty's?' snorts Neville.

'He's being funny. Pretends he coverts my suit!'

'Good job I didn't cancel the Irony completion meeting. Looks like you gotta busy day ahead!'

11

I've celebrated the contract signature over lunch with Terry and Dan at Le Caprice. Now I'm due for my assassination in Liberty's designer suit department. A sales assistant with glowing skin asks, 'Can I help you, Sir?' He holds out a two-piece suit and turns me to face a long swing mirror.

'I'm expecting someone,' I say. The assistant stalks off.

'Psst! Over here!' hisses a Latin voice. A familiar, swarthy face peeks around the door of a changing cubicle. Manslaughter, larceny, fraud. Help!

'Get in the next booth!' he hisses.

The sales assistant, unaware of my imminent demise, busies himself with paperwork at the till. An accomplice?

'Find something to try on,' orders Sonny. 'Getta fuckin' suit.'

I sidle sheepishly up to shop assistant Bruno (according to his badge) to warn him my life's in danger.

'Your friend not come?' he asks.

'I'd l-like to t-try one of your linen suits, please. Like the one I'm w-wearing.' I say nervously.

'One of ours, Sir, isn't it? Last year's model. We've three colours this season: light brown, dark brown, navy. What d'you fancy, Sir?' He glides over to clothes rails, I shuffle behind. 'You're a 38. Try this on, Sir, for size. Waist 32?'

He runs expert hands down labels, selects jacket and trousers, hands them to me, returns to the sales till. I carry the suit to a spare cubicle. It has a chair, coat hook, wooden hanger. Only a thin wall separates me from Sonny. I lock the door.

'Try it on!' he barks.

My hands shake as I remove my regular suit, hang it neatly on the hanger. Maybe he'll shoot me in cold linen? I ease myself into the designer creation.

Please, God, I should never have added a CBE to my name. I did it for a laugh. This isn't fair punishment for what was only a giggle. Please forgive me.

God replies, *'Not your only sin.'*

'My bar mitzvah speech?'

'Honour thy Father and Thy Mother...'

'Ready!' I call.

'Walk out, slowly. Look normal.' Whispers Sonny.

I stand facing Sonny's cubicle as Bruno approaches. Sonny's door bursts open. He strides out, opens his arms and guffaws, 'Surprise! Surprise!' He's wearing the same navy suit!

'Imagine I was gonna fill you full of lead?'

Bruno laughs nervously. Sonny addresses him. 'Thought I'd snuff him out in the cubicle, ha!' Turns to me. 'If I'd planned to bump yer off, do you think I'd do it in front of witnesses in *grande magazzino*, for Christsake?'

He straightens and buttons my jacket, pulls up my trousers, preens himself in a long mirror and says, 'We take both suits. I pay. *My* jacket needs taking in. *His* trousers are too long. How quickly you do alterations?'

Bruno's obsequious. 'If you come back the same time tomorrow, Sir, they'll both be ready.'

As he sticks pins in cloth, Sonny pinches my arm. 'You shoulda seen the look on yer mug!'

At the till, the assistant asks for Sonny's name. 'F-I-O-R-I!' he rattles off letters like shots from a machine-gun.

'F-I-O-R-I? That means flowers, doesn't it?' Bruno jots prices on an order form.

Sonny leans across the counter and jogs him. 'Hey, you're smart.' He taps him on the shoulder, 'I could use someone like you. Happy here?'

'Yes, Sir, very content.' Bruno doesn't look up.

Sonny extracts a smart wallet from his breast pocket, hands Bruno a business card. 'Change your mind, call me. Reverse charge.'

'Thank you, Sir.' Bruno places the card on the till, hands over the receipt, plus two alteration chits.

Sonny gives me my chit, puts receipts in his wallet, 'Where can I pick up a diet Coke?'

Bruno taps his fingers on the counter. 'There are several cafes in Carnaby Street, Sir.'

Sonny and I head towards the Marlborough Street exit, past panelled walls, a mock medieval arch, ties, cufflinks and stationery, out into hazy afternoon sun.

'Sonny, let's take a cab to *Bar Italia*. Any time pressure?'

He thumps my shoulder, 'Nope, sounds great. Meeting *una ragazza* for dinner, but now I'm all yours.' He buys Coke from a street stall and swigs it in the taxi. 'I'm parched, man.' He nudges me. 'Look at her! Nice piece of arse.' He gestures at a young hooker swinging down Old Compton Street.

'I'm married, about to have a baby...' I answer, trying to take my eyes off the girl.

We sit outside Bar Italia, on Frith Street, sipping cappuccinos. Inside, a crowd watches Italy thrash Romania on a giant TV. He cheers, 'Bravo!' points to a jazz club opposite. 'What's that dive like?' he asks.

'Ronnie Scott's? Never been there.'

'Say, maybe on my next trip?' he chuckles.

I can't stand the suspense. 'Sonny, I'm sure you didn't come all this way just to ogle the local talent.'

He adopts a serious look but can't mask the twinkle in his brown eyes. He straightens himself to lecture me. 'Stern, frankly, I'm disappointed in you,' he begins. 'You call me, *abbiamo fatto un affare*. I send you cash. Within hours, you're throwing it back in my face. But it could have been worse.'

'How?'

'You coulda kept the cash and run off to Guatemala.' He laughs again, 'Ever bin there?'

'No.'

'It's a shit hole! So now, I'm gonna have to work with that crook Grabball.'

Him again! My ghoul. God created the Heavens and the Earth. On the seventh day, He rested and on the

Eighth, he invented Grabball. Master of Terror! 'Grabball, but he's… '

Sonny delights in my astonishment. 'Apparently he failed to clinch a deal with your buddies at Irony but, this morning, he signed up with me.'

'You didn't wire him the cash, did you?'

'Stai scherzando!' he nudges me sharply as I'm about to sip coffee. Froth cascades down the side of my cup, into my saucer. 'He's *un piccolo dilinquente*. Been foolin' around with us for months. Thought he'd get better terms from Irony, but they blew him out yesterday.'

Is this another prank? 'Had lunch with Irony today. They never said anything.'

'You don't say?' Expressionless eyes.

'You didn't come over 'specially to see me, did you?'

He guffaws, 'You flatter yourself, though shopping with you's a gas. We trust you, Stern. We want to find a way to work with you.' He lays his elegant hand on my arm. 'We'll use Grabball 'til he gets greedy.'

'I can't work with you, Sonny. Know why? My lawyer did a search…'

'You trust your goddam *Inglese lawyer?'*

'Sure, he was in the RAF with Dad.'

He slaps his right thigh. 'Right! Stern, arrivederci. By the by, what's a CBE?'

'How d'you know?'

He sniggers, searches his wallet for British notes.

'Let me pay.' I fumble in my trouser pocket for change, place coins on the table.

Sonny grabs my hand, shakes it. 'Don't forget to pick up that suit, Stern. Wear it next time you're in New York. *Ciao!*' He hails a taxi and disappears.

I walk back to Old Compton Street, enter a red phone box with my mobile for privacy, call Dan Sharpstone.

'Dan, is it true you've ditched the deal with Grab-ball?'

Embarrassed silence. 'You're well-informed. Grab-ball's received investment from a U.S. outfit, Global Publishing. Heard of 'em?'

'Mmm.' I don't give the game away.

'By the way, all that stuff about Chinese walls is bull-shit,' Dan confesses.

12

TO LET: attractive redbrick industrial building, close to Camden Lock. I admire petunias in baskets hanging from iron hooks in the forecourt. A wild man opens the entrance door and yells, 'Can I help, Guv?' Baggy trousers, dirty sweatshirt, unlaced plimsolls.

'I'm enquiring about office accommodation.'

'You need to speak to Gavin; you'll find him in there.' He points to a small outhouse at the back of the car park.

I ring a bell. The intercom barks, 'Piss off, Des, you fuckin' misfit!'

I ring again. Hear a disembodied voice, 'Who the fuck..?'

'Good morning, Sir. I'm enquiring about office accommodation.'

'Come up!' the voice orders.

I ascend a narrow, wooden staircase to a dark room which overlooks the canal. An immaculate handsome man sits at a trestle table playing Pac Man on his laptop. Swept-back fair hair. Sharp, light grey suit. Pale pink shirt. Discrete green paisley tie. Gold signet ring, shiny black shoes. He looks at my scuffed brogues, faded jeans and sports jacket.

'Gavin Penhaligon,' he springs up, shakes my hand vigorously, 'Jolly good of you to pop in. How can I help?'

I sit in a trendy, leatherback chair. A stylish reading lamp shaped like a question mark sheds the only light. Architectural plans hang on every wall of his small loft.

'I need office space.'

He laughs. 'Then you've come to the right place. How big?'

'A thousand square feet would do it.'

'Minimum two thousand, I'm afraid,' he sighs.

'What a pity.' I reply. Two swans float along the canal. A drunk hurls a beer bottle at them. I wince.

'My building's empty at the moment, but there's a lot of interest. Twenty quid a square foot, plus rates and service. About twenty-five inclusive. Shall I show you around?'

He escorts me across the forecourt, bangs on the entrance. The door buzzes open. The wild man snoozes behind Reception. He jerks awake and asks, 'Everythin' all right, Guv?' Gavin strides past him. 'I'm Des, Security.' He rises from his desk, tucks his sweatshirt in his trousers, thrusts out a paw.

'Morning. I'm Ricky Stern.'

Gavin stands in the corridor, holds the door open. 'Shall we?'

As I pass, Gavin holds a finger up at Des who responds with, 'I love you too, Guv.'

'You'll have to forgive Des,' Gavin says. 'One of life's eccentrics. Where would we be without them?'

He shows me around the vast first floor loft. Beams, white brickwork, oak floorboards, brilliant view of the Lock. I'll partition it and build myself a mod office. I imagine my staff beavering away between massive, iron pillars on the ground floor.

'It's wonderful, Gav. But I can't afford two floors.'

'Too bad, old chap. We've had countless enquiries...'

'So, why's it still available?'

He softens his voice, conspiratorially. 'To be perfectly honest, by extraordinary coincidence, the recording studios opposite faxed an offer two minutes before you came.'

'Could I sublet them some of this?'

'Exactly. They have a new project. Anxious for space at any price. You could make a turn.' Sly wink-wink, know what I mean? 'Why don't you take your time, look round. I'll give you an hour. If I don't hear, I'll accept the other offer.' How incredibly generous. 'I'll be in my office. Des'll see you out.'

The recording studio will have the ground floor and we'll build a computer room on the first floor which will also be for me and my staff and our computer. I'll overlook the old Lock, admire swans. I've got the funds. Need room for expansion. What does God say?

'Be strong, for I Am The Lord and I shall not abandon those who believe in Me!'

Des paces Reception, eager puppy. He blocks my exit. 'Yer movin' in, Guv?' he barks.

Gavin suddenly appears through the front door, 'So Mr Stern, have you decided?'

Des creeps back to his desk to read The Sun.

'Okay, I'll take it. Once we've exchanged, may I contact the other party... about subletting?'

'But of course!' Reassuring hand on my arm.

Des delves into his rubbish bin, pulls out two scraps of paper and a chewed biro. Gavin and I exchange solicitor's details, shake hands.

Des hops over the desk, slaps our backs.

'Gerroff!' shouts Gavin, Des slinks off. 'We'll need references and a rent bond.'

'Rent bond?'

'Six months rent in escrow. Quite standard.'

This, plus the computer equipment deposit, will severely diminish our cash. Let's hope I can sublet.

Three weeks later, we are the proud occupants of a former brewery. I set myself up in one corner of the ground floor with an upturned crate for a desk, garden deck chair, mobile. Wait for furniture to be delivered and builders to erect glass partitions. Hammering and Cabling.

No news from the recording studio.

I hear swearing in the courtyard and head out to investigate. A group of Telecom engineers are in heated discussion with Gavin, immaculately attired amid the throng. Des leaps around, scared monkey. An engineer shouts at me, 'There he is!'

'What's the problem?' I ask.

'He's charging us fifty nicker a van for parking.'

'That right, Gav?' I ask.

He stands, feet wide apart, defiant. 'Certainly, your lease grants you three spaces. Now there's five vans, plus your car. Someone owes me for the three extra spots. That'll be £150.'

'Why, when the rest of the forecourt's empty?' I point at cobbles which sprout weeds. 'What if we move the extra vans?'

'Seems fair, Guv.' Des hops on the spot.

'Shut up, baboon,' Gavin shoves him away.

'Be reasonable,' I say. 'We'll move the vans onto meters. I'll check it doesn't happen again.'

He struts to his lair, shouts, 'Des, ger inside!' Des gallops off into the brewery.

As the vans leave the carpark, one by one, the first engineer says, 'That guy's a menace.'

Another shouts, 'Bleedin' moron.'

A third, 'Isn't he the clown in the toothpaste ad?'

'What ad?' I ask.

'Idiot with shiny teeth.'

Mr Molar is my landlord!

Let staff recruitment commence! My company will be different from GRAPE. There'll be no hierarchies, no office politics, no company cars. I place adverts in *Camden New Journal, The Guardian, The Lady*. I'm overwhelmed with replies and shortlist candidates under strict criteria: eccentricity, humour, good looks.

The first victim is a rotund Northerner in Reception, studying photos on Des' desk. Two workmen deliver a giant TV in a specially-commissioned, telephone-shaped yellow package, embossed with our company logo. They place it next to an emerald sofa.

'This is me being discharged from prison.' Des is pointing at a photo.

'Good morning,' I say.

Des's startled, 'Morning Guv, didn't see you there.'

I address the prospective candidate, 'You must be…' Christ, forgotten his damned name!

He extends his arm. 'Gary Plumber.' Thickset, ruddy cheeks, new dark suit, crumpled, scuffed black shoes. I lead him through crates, engineers, wires, planks, to a corner of the ground floor.

I sit in a deckchair, invite him to sit in one too with a crate between us. I pick up his application, 'So…' Bloody hell, what was his name?

'Gary, Gary Plumber,' he responds patiently. He gazes at the Amazonian Rainforest in a framed photo. My plan is to have an environmentally-friendly feel.

'So, Gary, you're working with Manchester City Council, yes? What makes you think you can handle being General Manager?'

He studies wires poking out of the ceiling and unconnected electricals. 'Want an honest answer?'

''Course.'

'You think administering parking fines for Manchester Council isn't linked to phone publishing? You're right.'

'Ah...' Time-waster. I shuffle the pile of applications, recall Julie and her Busy Lizzie plant, memories of mad times at the Commission.

'Mum has visions,' Oh no, a nutter indeed. 'She saw your advert in The Guardian and sent it to me. She saw me working with you.'

'She told *you* to work with *me?*' I ask in amazement.

He tries without success to lean forward in the deckchair but slides back heavily like a beached whale. 'She prophesied I'd be working with a guy who looks like Dustin Hoffman and a machine with many lights.' Hoffman's good-looking. I quite like this guy.

'That's perceptive. Our computer's got red lights; one goes on for each call. You techno-literate Gary?'

'I can't actually install computers if that's what you mean... but I do have an engineering degree.'

I perch on the window ledge. 'You'll need to put on the recordings, ensure they're updated, assigned to correct telephone numbers.'

'No prob,' he beams.

'You do realise this is a new company. Your job won't be half as secure as working in Manchester and anyway why do you want to move to The Big Smoke?'

'The girlfriend. I met her in Marbella and proposed last week. I'm moving into her flat in East London. I want to work for a dynamic, young company. Telephone publishing's the future. You seem to know what you're about.' Smart young lad.

'Right! When can you start?'

We agree on terms. I see him to the entrance where the next applicant, a long-legged blond, sits chatting to Des. 'Hi,' she says.

Gary looks her up and down and departs.

Des's smitten, can't take his eyes off her.

'You must be Tessa Compton.'

She flashes perfect teeth, green eyes. I lead her along the corridor, past two leering engineers drinking mugs of tea. 'You all right, love?' They chant in unison.

'Hello!' she smiles.

They gawk and elbow one another.

As we enter the open-plan office on the ground floor, she exclaims, 'Wow. It's super.'

A construction site: wires everywhere, workmen painting frenetically, electricians, cracked windows, crates, wrapped desks randomly placed. I beckon her to the guest deckchair. 'The deckchairs are temporary until proper chairs are delivered.'

She laughs and straightens her mini skirt. My blood pressure rises.

I pick up her interview form from my crate. 'Tessa, you've been working in a riding stable? What makes you think you could be our Marketing Manager?'

She wriggles against the deckchair fabric, it emits a scraping noise. 'I adore working with people.'

'But you've been working with horses.'

'I've also got a yoga diploma.' An engineer appears with a ladder to run a cable along the top of my partition. He eyes Tessa, drops the cable, disappears. 'I spent three years at night school.'

A yoga diploma! Be polite, let her go.

'You'll need to liaise with Cosmic Benny...' I continue anyway. I mean she's cute, right. Benny will like that...

She smiles, 'From Universe? He writes great *Starscopes!'*

I gaze into her eyes, can't help myself. 'We'll have several telephone quizzes. Terry Tomblin'll handle racing results. We'll have to butter up mags and TV stations. Ring-Inn's strategy is to develop joint ventures with both publishers and broadcasters.' My heart races.

The engineer returns with a mate and two ladders. They eye Tessa and march out.

'I'll contact editors and producers, persuade them to work with us.' She uncrosses her legs. 'I can definitely do that.'

'I'm sure that's true.' God, I have an erection. It'll be obvious when I stand up.

A workman carries in a rubber plant, positions it in a corner.

I pretend to glance through her form. 'Anything else you'd like to ask?'

She lowers her voice and eyelids, re-crosses her legs. 'How much will you pay me?'

'Twenty grand.'

'I'll need twenty-five to move to London.'

'Twenty-two and a half.'

'Twenty-five.'

I look at her perfect legs. 'Twenty-five it is.'

'You'd better smarten your ideas up, young man,' A battle-axe confronts me. Fifties, dyed brown hair, tweed business suit, matching fearsome brown handbag.

Des bobs up in the entrance door, embarrassed.

'He won't believe me when I say I've come for an interview,' she points at Des.

'Meg er... isn't it? I do apologise. I forgot to tell Des you were coming.' I shake her hand.

'Meg Walters,' she barks.

'My most humble apologies,' says Des then pops into the forecourt to water flower baskets. About to escort Meg to a deckchair, I see a giant stream spurt from Des's crutch. Then I realize he's got a hose clutched between his legs.

'Imbecile!' says Meg, pointing at Des.

She comments that the engineers obviously spend all day drinking tea, refuses to sit in a deckchair, insists on heaving over another crate, perches by my side.

'Meg, I hear you used to be a Bond Girl.' I look at her high cheekbones.

'In my twenties,' she snaps.

'Why do you want to be my PA?'

Her chest heaves and relaxes. 'Actually, I'd prefer to paint in Dorset but I'm supporting my kids through Uni. Yours is the only decent, local job I've seen. Working in Dulwich at the mo' in an Undertakers,' Sighs. 'Well, what do you want me to do?'

'Protect me from Cosmic Benny...' She grimaces. 'Get me into *Le Caprice*, fix appointments with scary people, make cups of tea, type the occasional letter, keep me amused.'

'I can't promise the last one.'

'Do your best.'

'Scouts' Honour!' She smiles wanly, salutes.

The only experienced hire is our Financial Controller. I hire him from an agency for freelance accountants. Utter disaster! Gary catches him lurking outside Irony offices, clutching a beer bottle. I replace him with Basil, who we recruit at great expense from a Telecom subsidiary.

We're all set to Go!

13

As Launch Day approaches, anxious Gary tears around the basement computer room waving a screwdriver. Tessa *schmoozes* "artistes."

Meg makes phone calls. 'I'm certain Mr Stern would like to meet you for lunch... I'll check, can you please hold.' She covers the receiver and shouts through the partition. 'You do want to take the manager of the Odeon Swiss Cottage to lunch with you, Benny and your bank manager, don't you?'

I dash out to confront her, 'No, why should I?'

'I found this on my desk.' She hands me a scrap of paper. *Phone... Bank Manager. Manager Odeon Swiss Cottage. Lunch Benny.*

'Meg!'

'Yes, Ricky.'

'I must phone my bank to arrange an overdraft. I'll give the Odeon manager a bollocking for messing up a ticket reservation. I've got to lunch Benny. He's moaning 'bout money and we haven't even launched.'

She puts hand to face, 'Whoops!'

'Is anyone there?' shouts a voice from the phone handset which is resting on a cheese sandwich, wrapped in clingfilm.

Launch Day. Universe and Racing On publish our numbers. Little red lights flash on our computer. A machine works out how much money we've taken. By the end of the day it's £1000. Frighteningly successful!

After work, we decamp to the *Brasserie* for our Launch Party. Marco, a tall Uruguayan giraffe, welcomes us. 'Meester Stern. The lovely Meg and equally lovely Tessa. I believe we are fellow spirits.' Another nutter?

The restaurant bar is packed. Tessa rushes up, presses a wet kiss on my cheek. 'Ricky, isn't this exciting? Everyone's coming, even Glen Hopkins, Promotions Director of Universe.'

'How did you wangle that?'

'He liked the sound of my voice...'

Terry, immaculate in a navy blazer, pushes his way through the throng. Drinks orange juice. 'Fuckin' marvellous! That's Charlie Dimmock, editor of Universe.' He points to a short bloke with wispy white hair, drinking with Gary. They prop up the bar, boozing. Gary clutches his screwdriver.

'Glen Hopkins, Universe Promotions Manager, is coming too!' I shout above funky jazz.

'Glen fuckin' Hopkins?' Terry's face contorts.

'Yeah, what's the problem?'

'He and Charlie loath one another. Jeezuz!' He heads towards Charlie and Gary.

Cosmic Benny approaches, drinking a fluorescent cocktail to match his tunic. He holds a joint in the air, above the heads of the crowd. 'Hey, man! Great to see yer... you're lookin' good.'

Bloody liability! 'Benny, we're in a *Brasserie*, not a *souk*. Put that out.'

'Chill out, man.' He stubs the joint out in a glass, 'Rick, we must talk.'

'Can't it wait?' Where the hell's Meg? She's paid to protect me from hip lunatics.

He crushes me against the wall, stands over me, fist on the wall blocking my escape. 'No, man. Get this. I ain't bin paid yet.'

Putrid breath, yellow teeth. 'You're on a royalty. You don't get paid 'til we do.'

He edges closer, 'Don't get all technical with me, man. I need dosh *now*. No dough, no show!'

I duck under his armpit, yell, 'Baz!' Basil's drinking Evian with Mel Silver and Dan Sharpstone. Triplets in matching dark suits. He disengages himself and struggles through the hordes.

'Baz, you've met Cosmic Benny.' Basil nods at the hippy. 'He needs an advance on his royalty payments. Can you sort out something?'

Baz grimaces. 'Like how much?'

'£1k a month,' I propose.

'In cash!' Benny rolls a joint.

'Cash?' Basil's eyebrows arch.

'Yeah, why not?' Benny stuffs the paper, licks it, lights up.

'You'll have to sign an indemnity, to protect us from the Revenue,' replies Basil.

'What's an indemnity, man?' he inhales, stumbles, then recovers.

'To say you're responsible for your own PAYE.'

Benny turns to me, slurs, 'Rick, this nut's fuckin' me mind.'

'Benny, it's simple. You're on our payroll. You want cash, you sign a form.'

He inhales, 'This is too much, man. I jes want me lolly.' Eyes glazed, voice raised.

Tessa rushes by, 'Hopkins's arrived, let's go meet him.' She drags me away. I leave Basil and Benny to slog it out.

A BMW, number plate GH1 draws up. Hopkins strides through the door. Media man, gold neck chain, blue shirt, tanned, handsome. 'Tessa Compton here?' he asks Marco.

'Hi, I'm Tessa. This is Ricky Stern.' He shakes my hand but looks at Tessa.

'Aren't you going to introduce me?' Interrupts a stranger behind me.

Matt Bloody Grabball! Exterminate! Exterminate! What the fuck's he doing here? God help me. No reply. 'Err, Glen Hopkins, Matthew Grabball.'

'From Phoneworks,' Grabball smiles. Grabball matches Hopkins in a red jacket, black trousers, copper wristband. Hopkins will think the bugger works with me.

Marco interrupts with a cordless phone.

'Meester Stern. Urgent call for you from your wife.'

I grab the phone.

'Darling, you'd better come home right now. My waters have broken. We'll have to drive to the hospital.'

Bloody hell! 'I'll leave right now, sweetheart.' Stunned, I turn to Tessa, 'Susie's having my baby. Must go. Hold the fort for me.'

'Yes... yes.' Distracted. She rallies, smiles sadly, wanders towards the bar where Hopkins and Grabball are locked in conversation.

My son was born last night, but there's no rest for the wicked. I lunch at *The Brasserie*.

'Meester Stern, Welcome back. Congratulations! They're waiting for you at your usual table.' Marco sports a green tank top, jeans and shades strung on a chain around his neck.

My team are seated at a window table. I squeeze in between Tessa and Terry below a painting of a Spaniard in a poncho and white hat.

'Ricky!' Tessa kisses my cheek. Golden hair sticks to my face. 'Congrats! How much did he weigh?'

'What?'

'How much did the baby weigh?'

Oh, him! '7.10, or was it 10.7? Can't remember.'

'Ricky, honestly!'

'Have you ever had a baby, Tessa? No, well, it's traumatic. God knows how I'm gonna sleep when Seth comes out of the hospital. Apparently, Seth was Susie's grandfather's nickname.'

'Don't you get a say?' asks Tessa.

'I chose the second name, Orlando.'

'Seth Orlando Stern!' scoffs Terry.

'Watch out Terry,' I nudge him, 'or I'll invite you to the *bris*, next week. That's the circumcision.'

'Circumcision, yuk!' Gary squirms in his seat.

I order pasta. Terry, Basil and Gary gnaw steaks. Tessa has a tuna salad. Terry insists on a bottle of champagne.

'How did our first week go, revenue-wise, Baz?' I ask.

He takes out a creased folded A4 sheet from his shirt pocket, unfolds it, places it between breadbasket and champagne glass. 'Sales £8k, loss £3k. Roughly on budget.'

We're losing money. Panic stations.

Gary sees I'm disappointed. 'It's only the first week, Rick,' he says, eyes to heaven.

Tessa puts her arm around me, rocks me gently. Nice perfume. I gently release myself. 'Now Tessa, what happened after I left the party?'

Terry jumps in. 'What fuckin' happened? You should 'ave seen it, the whole place was mobbed. Charlie Dimmock from Universe...'

I cut him off, 'That's great, Tel, but when I left Hopkins and that sod Grabball were in cahoots together. Tessa, tell me what happened?'

She lowers her eyes, mutters, 'Hopkins propositioned me.'

'So?' I ask, praying she didn't react.

'He left with Grabball. They went off to a sleazy nightclub.' Oh, terrific! I host an expensive do so my main competitor can run off with my primary client.

'Bye, bye Universe business,' says Gary glumly.

'Well, why didn't *you* sleep with him?' snaps Tessa to Gary. 'Instead of getting pissed.'

He reddens, 'I'm not that sort of pansy boy. I was keeping Charlie company. He's now our only ally on the paper.'

'Now, now children,' I interject. 'Terry, it's time we worked on National Sentinel for them to also take our racing results service.'

'I'm ahead of you, Rick,' says Terry. 'We start a racing joint venture next month.'

'Fantastic! Grabball's made one mistake. He doesn't have a racing division and, most important, he doesn't have a gem like you, Tel.' Terry turns beetroot. 'You, Terry, are Ring-Inn's lynchpin.'

Pass the sick bag.

14

Grabball's glitzy Phoneworks consists of three offices with green-tinted glass doors, an open plan section and tropical, potted plants. Clone of Ring-Inn. It's even up the road from us next to Bar Spagna.

The receptionist takes Terry and me into Grabball's office. Coffee table, phone, three chairs, nicked Telecom promotional poster, desk-less. His hair has highlights, a jazzy blue shirt, snakeskin trousers. Wouldn't be let through the door of Telecom.

Grabball looks up from the Financial Times, throws it on the table, mutters, 'Thanks for coming. Sit.' No handshake. 'Tea, coffee?' The receptionist leaves with our order.

Grabball looks into the middle distance, fiddles with a rubber band. 'I gather we have a mutual friend, Stern... '

'Sonny Fiori?' I ask.

'Yeah, Sonny... Listen, we could fight this one out. Or come to mutually satisfactory accommodation,' replies Grabball.

Terry and I glance at one another. 'What sort of accommodation?' I ask.

Grabball stares directly at me, narrows his eyes. 'We could pay you to go away.'

'Not interested.'

'You couldn't afford him,' interjects Terry.

Grabball glares. 'How would *you* know, Paddy?'

Terry opens his legs, hands on hips, leans forward, 'Because we've only just begun, to quote a fuckin' song.'

Grabball scowls. 'Stern, we're prepared to buy out your shareholding for £300k.'

'And Irony?'

Grabball folds his arms. 'They'd stay in. We can use their dough and contacts. We'll merge the two companies. But we want you Out!'

'And me?' asks Terry.

'You're harmless. You stay with us.'

Terry sits upright, unbuttons his blazer, fiddles with his red tie. 'And what if I don't wanna fuckin' work for you lot?'

'Then no deal,' Grabball scorns.

'No deal anyway, Matt.' I start to rise.

'Sit!' he orders.

The receptionist places drinks on the low table.

'Stern, I want to make myself perfectly clear. We have big plans and we're gonna implement 'em. I'm offerin' you 300 fuckin' k to disappear from my life. You're an irritant. Without you, we'd have had the market sewn up. But you came along an' spoilt our party.'

'Like you didn't spoil mine?'

He grimaces. '300k to disappear. If you turn it down, we'll stop at nothing. Geddit?'

'Tel, let's go,' I say.

On the pavement outside, Terry whines, 'You could have strung him out a bit. I wanted to finish my coffee.'

We walk along the canal path and join the queue in Primrose Patisserie. We order food and find a place at an old sewing machine which serves as a table. 'Jezus!' says Terry. 'Grabball's trouble with a capital "T".'

A lanky vagrant, reeking of pot, pulls up a chair. 'Mind if I join you?' asks Cosmic Benny.

The waitress thumps down three cappuccinos and two Danish pastries.

'What brings you to trendy Primrose Hill?' asks Terry.

Benny's thin hand trembles as he sips. 'Somefin' on me mind.'

'What's that, Benny?'

'Dough.' He's ghostly pale with thick stubble, red eyes, unkempt hair.

'Well, you're in a bakery!' Terry quips.

Benny grabs a Danish, takes a bite, coughs. 'I'm bloody skint. Got this call.'

'Don't tell me. Matt fuckin' Grabball,' I say.

Benny, spreads out his arms, 'Gee, man, you psychic?'

I scoff the Danish, 'How much did he offer?'

'I'm freaked, man.'

'How much?' I ask.

'Two grand,' he replies.

'A month, I presume?'

'Ricky, I trust you. This guy, his voice, it was... weird vibration.' Quivering fingers raise his coffee cup. 'Need a smoke.' He fumbles in his threadbare jacket for *Rizla*.

Terry grasps the pack, throws it on the table. 'Not in here, Sunshine. It's no-smoking.' He points to a notice above the cash machine.

A couple opposite glare at the *Rizla*.

'Benny, listen,' I say. 'We're paying you one grand retainer in cash against royalties. I'm not being blackmailed. You want to work for that weasel Grabball, then good luck to you. Stay with me and I'll see you're paid on time. What's it to be?'

'Stay with you,' he mutters half-heartedly into his lukewarm cappuccino.

'That's settled. Now you help me. Grabball's offered me a small fortune to sell my shares in Ring-Inn. He wants me to bugger off. You're the Astrologer, what shall I do?'

Benny rubs his stubble, attempts to concentrate. 'Man, that's a tough call. Got some paper?' Terry offers him a paper napkin and a biro. 'When were you born?' Benny asks.

'3.15 a.m. September 18th Middlesex Hospital.' The angels rejoiced; a great conman was born.

He scrawls mysterious hieroglyphics, gazes at his handiwork. 'Hang on in there, man!

'Phew!' Terry exclaims.

'One last thing,' says Benny. 'Beware the man from the West.' He lurches out of the door into Regent's Park Road.

'What the fuck did that mean?' asks Terry.

'Maybe Sonny... But don't tell me you're a believer in all that stuff.'

Terry gets distracted. 'Jezuz, Rick, he's barefoot,' pointing to Benny in the street outside.

'So was Jesus.'

I drag my mouse across my desk. A sharp pain shoots down my side, my neck locks and I stumble out to Meg, tilting sideways. 'I'm crippled, help. Do something!'

'Let me help!' says Tessa. 'Can we use your office?' I open the door and she glides in. She beckons me to my Persian rug and runs her hand down my spine. She comments on my stooped posture. 'Let's start by standing, shall we? Take off your jacket and shoes. Loosen your belt. You're very tense.' She places her hand on the nape of my neck. 'You're too focused, too out there. Take off your specs.' I lay them next to my model aeroplane. 'I'm going to try an Alexander exercise. Let's see if we can straighten your poor back. Lie on the rug. I need three books.'

'Where did you learn all this stuff?' I ask.

'Yoga, I told you. I have a diploma.'

She picks up *Siddhartha, The Trial* and *The Godfather* and places them under my neck for support. 'Raise your legs, knees pointing to the ceiling.' She gently stretches my right arm, left arm, right leg, left leg. My pain diminishes. She squats, pushes down on my knees. Fair hair dangles above my crotch.

She straddles me, sucks my hot dog, exposes a black lace bra. We roll over, groan ecstatically.

Suddenly, the goods lift door snaps open. The vague outline of a man in uniform tumbles out. 'Oh! Excuse me, Sir. Where am I?'

Tess leaps up. 'The Chief Executive's office.'

'What do you want?' I bark.

The blurred face above me barks, 'Fire Prevention Officer, Sir. Mandatory inspection.'

I struggle to my feet, grope for my specs. The bald officer's suspicious, but Tess isn't flustered.

'Officer, I can explain...' I stammer.

He shunts the Fire Escape door open. 'Everything appears to be in order, Sir.' He smirks, 'Well, I'll leave you two love-birds to your devices!' He disappears down the wrought-iron stairway.

I put on my shoes, fasten my belt and congratulate Tess on her healing powers. My neck's free from pain and I can stand upright.

'I love it here,' Tessa says, 'especially the view over the Lock, and your toys.' She strokes a brass *Ganesh* and a balsa wood model aeroplane on my desk.

Let's run away to Camden Lock Hotel and fuck all night.

I stand inches from her and admire her swan's curved neck. She fiddles self-consciously with my card file, waiting for me to make a move. Instead, I stare guiltily at the photo of Susie cradling Seth, balanced on the windowsill.

Meg calls, 'Susie wants to know whether you want gnocchi or fishcakes for supper.'

'Fishcakes!'

Tessa glances at her watch. 'Home time then.' She turns and sails through the door.

Meg shouts, 'Cosmic Benny's on his way up.'

'Which way?' I ask, anxiously.

'The main stairs.'

'I'm outta here. See ya tomorrow.'

I grab my coat, open the Fire Escape and tear down the iron stairs into the forecourt. Bump head-on into Tessa.

'Where's the fire?'

'I'm running away,' I reply.

'Drink?'

Jesus! I'm out of my depth. 'I'm... '

She's got a sad look. 'It's Okay. Another time, maybe.'

'Wait, just a minute...'

She sits on the entrance steps, while I walk out of earshot and call Susie on my mobile. 'Darling,' I say, 'Be a bit late. Quick drink with clients.'

Seth whimpers in the background. 'Clients? You're babysitting. Girls' night out. I have been looking forward to it for weeks.'

Fuck I forgot. Wish she'd allow us a babysitter. Can't get out of it. I glance at Tessa, she waves at me.

'Terry'll cover,' I lie to Susie.

I wander over to Tessa. 'I'm sorry, it's an important new client.'

'What about the fishcakes?'

'Let's do it another evening.'

'Won't hold my breath,' she replies and walks out of the gates as I unlock my car door and clamber in.

Lunchtime the next day, I sit on a bench on Primrose Hill with my sarnies. Beneath me, Canary Wharf, St. Pauls, London Zoo Aviary. Benny climbs up the hill. Rainbow tunic and sandals, stench of dope. He wears a ridiculous black hat with a small flashing red neon light. Does this guy have a life? He's seems to spend the whole time shadowing me.

Sits beside me. 'You hate me, don't you?'

'No, Ben, I love you.'

We gaze at a tramp combing grass with a metal detector. It bleeps, he bends, picks up an object, drops it into a canvas bag.

'What do you want, cash?'

'Hey, man, that's not cool. Wanted to bond.'

'Since you're here, let me give you some advice. Stop taking those bloody drugs.'

'What drugs?'

'Ben, don't play games. If you don't get yourself together soon, Universe'll fire you. Have you done your recordings for tomorrow yet?'

He pulls my jacket sleeve; I flick off his hand.

'It pissed me off when you fled down the fire escape, Stern,' he says.

'Go back and do your job. I promise I'll be back after lunch and we'll have a nice chat.'

He floats downhill. Suddenly, I have a premonition and jog back to the office. Meg and Accounts are there, staring at the Lock excitedly. I fight my way to the window. Twenty police in yellow jackets have lined up punters and dealers with their backs to the wall, hands behind their heads. In the middle is a familiar Technicolor figure, Cosmic Benny under arrest.

I have a new profession—writing horoscopes.

Tessa rushes into my office clasping an Evening Standard. She throws it down on my desk. The headline reads, 'Universe astrologer arrested.'

'Oh, no!' I pick up the paper. 'There's a photo. How did they get that?' I skim the text. Local businessman, Matt Grabball was passing with his camera! 'The sod. It means Benny's had it. How are we doing with those horoscopes?'

Terry bounds in and slouches on the sofa. 'Listen to this. Hello, Taurus. Take a chance, it's your lucky day. You'll find love in unexpected quarters. Lucky number, 5. Lucky colour, creative green.'

'It's inspired.'

Tess sits in full lotus on the floor, reads from her notebook. 'Hi, Pisces. You're in an emotional whirlpool but soon things will go your way. Do something for someone else today. Lucky number, 3. Lucky colour, blood red.'

'We'll need a voice.'

Terry points at Tessa. 'Tantric Tessa!'

'It'll cost you,' she laughs.

'Don't worry, love. I'll chose a sexy freelancer. We'll say Benny's on holiday!' says Terry.

Six weeks later...

My phone rings. 'I'm not doing anything 'til I've solved this fuckin' crossword.' I slam the receiver down and gaze at The Guardian on my desk. The phone rings again, I grab it, shout, 'What is it, Meg?'

'May I bring a surprise in?'

'If you must.' I reply.

My office door bursts open. Meg shouts, 'Dah-dah!' with a flourish.

A smart young man in a trendy black suit, gold stud in one ear bounces in? 'Hey, man!'

Is it a bird, is it a bloody 'plane? No, it's bloody Benny. 'Good grief! What's happened to you? You look like an estate agent.'

His head droops, 'That's a cruel jibe, man.'

I take his arm and gesture to the sofa, 'Take a seat. Drink?'

Meths, beer, liquid heroin? He clasps my hand, squeezes and releases it, then gazes over the Lock. 'I was arrested there, man. It changed me bleedin' life... You gotta peppermint?'

Herb tea! Maybe he's Jesus, after all. *'Your errant son redeemed.'* I'll ring Ted at the Electricity Commission later and say I have a new recruit for his Bible studies.

'I'll pop out and buy some,' sighs Meg.

He settles down on the sofa. What a transformation! He's tanned, rested, glowing. Neatly trimmed blond hair. No stench of incense. Chic after-shave.

'What's this all about, Benny? You haven't joined 'Jews for Jesus,' have you?'

His smooth, healthy face wrinkles. 'That a cool band?'

'Never you mind. Talk to me.'

He unbuttons jacket, arms stretched out behind him, 'Well, after the drugs bust things went pretty bleak, man. Banged up in a fuckin' cell. Then they hustle me to the back entrance and shove me into the back of a goddamed black hearse.'

'A hearse?'

'Fuckin' coffin carrier. Thought I was on me way to meet me Maker.' He points skywards.

'His Time is yet to come,' saith the Lord.

'Continue...' I command.

'Well, the hearse was a disguise.'

'It was really a jeep?'

He smiles wryly, 'No, man, it was a stretched Limo. Lounge seats, bar, flowers, the lot. And bleedin' Charlie Dimmock from Universe is sitting there sippin' champagne.'

'What a surprise.'

'So I ask Charlie for a drink and 'e says, 'You've been bad. You're in serious shit, kid. We're payin' for you to get cleaned up.' They take me to this grotty place. The Nunnery. Full o' creepie dudes, hookers, junkies, popstars. They lock me in, man. At first, I beg 'em to send me back to the nick. At least you get great dope there. Then I get withdrawals. Spiders, accountants, little green men. Then I see the light. That there's more to life than Archway Road.'

'And?'

'After three weeks, Charlie visits me. I'm reformed, I say have me back. He says he'll think 'bout it. Then that damned hearse comes again. This time to Universe HQ. There's a group of weirdos in starched white coats. They take me blood, ask me riddles. Suddenly they split and our Charlie appears. He says they're gonna re-launch me as a model for today's youth.'

A toss-up between him and Prince Charles. 'You? A role model? You're joking!'

'Don't mock me, man. I'm serious. I'm clean now... an' I met my dream chick in rehab.'

He pulls a photo of a beauty from his lapel pocket.

'You lucky bastard. She's young enough to be your daughter.'

His face is serious, 'Rita and me, we were meant for each other.'

Cosmic Benny and Rehab Rita.

15

'Mel, I've had a disturbing statement from Urban Mortgages. Think they've made a dreadful accounting error.'

He clears papers, shines table lamp in my face, 'Tell me everyzink!' he says in a mock German accent.

I push the lamp away, 'Well, they insist I have an outstanding loan of £250k. Our flat's only worth £250K, and the bloody mortgage was £230k.'

'I'll fish out your mortgage details.' He opens a metal filing cabinet, extracts a green file with a white label: *Urban Mortgages/Stern*. Slumps back in his seat, and reads. 'You have what they call a negative equity situation.'

'What the hell does that mean? I'm skint.'

He sketches a house on his pad, a pound sign and a downward arrow, 'Ultimately it means your house is worth less than your mortgage. QED.' He hurls his biro at an inch of desk space and it collides with a roll of Polos. 'I told you all this when I came round. You have a fixed repayment policy. You repay the same each month, but interest rates today are sky-high. In simples, your additional interest has been added to outstanding capital.' He scrawls *Selfridges* on a blotter, mumbles, 'Remember toaster.'

'Don't tell me I'm paying bloody interest on top of the interest!' I retort.

He replaces the file, bangs the cabinet drawer shut. ''Fraid so, and according to my calculations, the capital sum you owe is increasing by 1,000 quid per month.'

I gasp. 'I'm going bloody broke! I don't have savings. I've got less than ten grand in the world.'

'Technically, you don't even have that, because it's on loan from your mortgage company.'

I have a panic attack. 'How come *you* let me get into this mess?'

He sighs. 'Ricky, you said you wanted to re-mortgage your apartment at any cost. In order that you could close the Irony investment, remember? I told you not to do it!'

I squirm. 'Yeah, but you also knew I'd blame you if it didn't work out.' He turns his eyes to heaven and shrugs. 'You're my accountant, do something, for God's sake!'

'It is easier for a camel to enter the Kingdom of Heaven, than for a rich man to thread a needle,' says God.

'And if the company falters...?' I ask.

'Then you could end up working for those loan sharks for the rest of your life,' he replies glumly.

The phone market's still growing, but soon it'll reach saturation. We're neck-and-neck with Grabball's Phoneworks, but he's a devious bastard. He'd do anything to ruin me. Steal business, bribe, sabotage our equipment, tap phones. He might even have me bugged. I glance furtively at Mel's phone.

At last, Mel says something useful. 'Ricky, you want my advice? Quit while you're ahead. Find a buyer for your business.'

'Wow, Mel, this is a huge shock!' Fine mess he got me into.

'Don't leave it too long. At the moment, your business is attractive, but things change overnight. I wouldn't like to see you working for papa-in-law!'

'Mr Fiori on the line,' says Meg.

I calculate I can survive four months before defaulting on my mortgage. 'Put him through.'

'Hey, Ricky. How's it going?'

I use my perky voice, 'Great, Sonny. How's your investment in Phoneworks?'

'That crook Grabball's doing a great job for us. Smart operator, but we're keen to cooperate with your good self.'

'Afraid it won't be possible.'

'Oh, I wouldn't be too sure 'bout that. I hear you've gotta cash situation.'

I might as well place an advert in Ham and High or The New York Times.

'Sonny, that's absurd.'

'Ricky, Ricky! *Diceme* pal, who you think owns Urban Mortgages.'

Oh, my God!

'I'll be in town next week. Buy you a coffee at The Brasserie.'

And make me an offer I won't be able to refuse.

Marco at The Brasserie sports a green tank top, blue jeans, matching plimsolls. His shiny head towers above me. 'Meester Stern, it is late. You lost track of time?' he shouts above brash Brazilian jazz. He leads me past a blazing fireplace, grill, two fake blondes.

I pass Benny and his companion. 'Hey, man! Thought you'd be tucked up in bed by now.' says Benny.

He beckons me to join them, introduces his fiancée Rita. She sips Evian. 'Heard all 'bout you,' she giggles.

'How's it goin', man?' asks Benny.

I feel a pain in my chest, 'Oh, under some strain at the mo.'

He hugs Rita to his chest, says, 'Ricky needs help from above.'

'God?' I ask.

'Witches!' He flicks through his Filofax, scribbles a number on his napkin.

Marco objects, 'Meester Benny! This is not paper; it is pure linen.'

Benny thrusts me the napkin. 'These dudes are magic.'

I scan it. 'A spell Benny, you kidding?'

Marco places a giant paw on my shoulder, 'Meester Stern...' and beckons me to a corner table in a dining area next to a palm tree.

Sonny in a huge fedora and navy suit weaves his way through diners. 'Ricky, you're wearing our suit.' He bear hugs me, sits. 'Great discrete table.' Sonny hurls his hat at the face of an iron Aztec head, doubling as a lampshade, misses.

Marco retrieves it, hangs it on a metal hook. 'Drinks?'

'Diet Coke for my friend and spritzer for me please.' I reply.

Sonny waits for Marco to go to the bar, 'So, my friend, how's life?'

'I've mortgaged to... to... you, but at least business is still booming!'

'You're sad! I want only happy. Name's not Sonny for nuffin.'

'Have you had time to look at the menu?' asks a cute waitress. I order Salad Nicoise. Sonny, a rare fillet steak.

'You don't have many options. And you 'aven't got cash stashed away, right?'

'Where we going with this Sonny?'

'We'll have effective control of your shareholding... But I like you. Stern, always have. I gotta proposition for you. We'll buy out your shares for $750k and freeze your outstanding mortgage at £250,000.'

'That'd be it for me? I'd walk away?'

Sonny thumps my back, 'A man as gifted as you? No!'

'I'm not working for that shit Grabball whatever happens.'

'Grabball'll be history.'

'You'd fire him?'

The waitress brings our meal. I toy with croutons as he tucks into his rare steak.

'Let's focus on you. You'd work for us!' he says between bites.

'No deal.' I say without thinking. Have I gone mad?

'As you make your bed, so shall thy lie,' says God.

Silence. Sonny chucks his fork onto the tablecloth, grabs his napkin, sobs. Fat tears run down sallow cheeks.

I place my hand on his arm. 'Sonny? Is it something I said?'

He takes a deep breath, pats his face with his napkin, blows his nose on it, says, 'Imagine a cold winter's evening at Thanksgiving. I arrive, keys in hand to eject you, your wife, your beautiful baby. Homeless in fog and snow.'

'You could always help me out.'

He looks me straight in my eyes, 'Oh no, buddy… I couldn't possibly do that.'

Arrive at Mel's office.

'Won't be a tick.' Mel rushes through Reception. 'Sorry to keep you, Rick.'

I sit in a creaky black armchair. Yesterday's FT, outdated Hellos, Property Gazette, and Accountancy Age rest on coffee table. Peeling paintwork, faded carpet, ancient chandelier. Musty smell.

'Enter!'

'Bold painting,' I say to red and blue geometric squares, hung by his office window.

'An old client gave it me. Stamford Hill at sunset.'

'Bit *risqué* for you.'

'In lieu of fees, Ricky. What could I do?' He tips back his seat, 'Lucky *you* didn't marry my daughter. You're in what we Accountants' term a ruddy pickle.'

'How can business be powering ahead while I'm in this shit.'

'I warned you, quit while you're ahead. Sell your shareholding for around £300k.'

'Who to?'

'Try Universe.'

'It's run by that megalomaniac Richard Sargant.'

'What, the Czech guy?'

'Yep.'

'Beggars can't be choosers, Ricky,' he sighs.

16

As I head for my office, Meg grabs my arm. 'Ricky, something ghastly's happened. I've discovered I'm Jewish.' She's tinted her hair sepia to match her brown cardigan and black dress.

I'm on a mission to save my poor family from destitution, not indulge in a counselling session. 'It's all true, in Mother's diary.' She shuts an ancient red notebook with stained brown pages, gently lays it on her desk. A cloud of dust rises in a shaft of sunlight from a dormer window.

'You'll have to call people "mean" rather than "Jewish" now.' Can't stand here chatting to her. Got to chair a management meeting.'

I grab her phone and press the broadcast button. 'Attention Management! Our meeting has been delayed by five minutes due to Meg's identity crisis. Please make your way slowly to the Boardroom.' I place my hand on her shoulder. 'Stop worrying, start tidying. Terry's clear desk policy has been in place for two weeks. Yours looks as if a bomb's hit it.'

I scamper down two flights of stairs, along the corridor to the Boardroom. I feel self-important as I place myself at one end of the vast table, to face a painted Jerusalem Temple. Was I a moneychanger, priest or harlot in my last life?

'Ye were the original Scapegoat,' mocks God.

Gary arrives in a smart, pressed, suit. Then Terry, Basil, Tessa.

Susie suggested I take more interest in staff, stop looking at them as a drain on profits. 'Have a good holiday in Mull, Gary?'

'I'm fuckin' livid.' Gary kicks the table. 'Someone's tidied my desk. Can't find a thing.'

'I warned you before you left. Meg's got your stuff in three cardboard boxes—except for this!' I pull out a four-foot rocket, from under the desk.'

'Fuckin' hell! He could've blown us all up!' shouts Terry.

Gary looks sheepish.

I dump the firework on the table. 'Luckily, Tel, your clear desk policy saved us. Were you planning a trip to the moon, Gary?'

He reddens, squirms. 'Err, it was a spare from the summer party. I meant to take it home for the kids.'

'A year ago? Take it home, tonight!' I shove it across the table. 'Don't let me see it here again! Baz, this week's results please.'

Basil stops doodling on management reports, reads, '£100k.'

'Previous week?'

'£104k.'

'You sure it's not the wrong way round?'

'Nope.' He slides me an annotated chart.

'But that's impossible,' I proclaim. 'The revenue always goes up. It's a law of nature. Look, 50 weeks uninterrupted growth.'

'Overheads this week?'

'£85k.'

'Previous week?'

'£80k.'

'Chart.' Basil slides me a chart, distributes copies. 'Profit's tumbling. At this rate, we'll be losing money in a few months. We must do something.' I proclaim.

'But it's only one week,' says Gary, somewhat perplexed.

'One week to you Gary is a lifetime to me. Why's it happening?'

Terry chimes in. 'It's the fuckin' competition! Everyone's seen 'ow well our racin' services are doin' and they're all undercutting us. The sods.'

Gary stares at a blonde in a mini-skirt, waiting in the forecourt, 'Gary, how's the TV Comp going?'

He jerks to attention. 'Stalled by another week. The Television Authority won't allow a car prize. The prize value's gotta be less than a grand.'

Tessa raises her arms towards the ceiling and stretches, 'Tess, this isn't a yoga session.'

She lays her hands on her lap, says, 'Financial information and horoscopes are steady but pop quizzes – in fact all quizzes – are falling. Increase advertising spend?'

'What, spend even *more* money? We can't. We're in crisis. We'll suspend the meeting for one hour. During that time, I'll give you one task each. Ready? Gary, ring Morning Time, ask them to replace the car with five Sony Walkmans. Tell them they'll make more money that way. As a personal favour to me, to do a trial before our next management meeting.'

'Right on.' Gary extracts a battered pink envelope from his jacket pocket, scribbles instructions below a red-inked heart.

'Baz, I want you to work through some projections with Gary, to see if the TV work will bring us back on budget next month.'

'Okey-dokey,' he responds.

'Tess, we need a quick fix. I have a brill idea. What goes on forever and costs no money?'

'Sex,' she replies.

Cheeky.

'The Speaking Clock.' Terry frowns, Tess is puzzled, Basil bashes at his calculator, Gary chokes. I continue regardless, 'We'll have an Alternative Speaking Clock voiced by that Page 3 girl. What's her name?'

'Lucinda Shaw,' sniffs Tessa. 'Her agent's Paula Vickers. Paula and I had a drink last week. What do you actually want Luce to say?'

'I want her to speak the time and twenty catchy phrases like: Wakey-wakey! It's 6 o'clock, or Put a soddin' move on, it's 8.33.'

'You sure, Rick?' asks Tess, concerned for my sanity. Gary and Terry shake their heads in dismay.

'Tel, I want to give you your assignment in private. You stay behind. Everyone else, we'll reconvene at noon. Good luck!'

They file out dutifully.

Terry waits for the door to close, then hisses. 'Alternative Fuckin' Speaking Clock? You gone fuckin' crazy?'

I sit on the Board table. 'It's a smokescreen. Tel, I'm entrusting you with a mission of the utmost importance. It's time to sell the biz. I've got mortgage problems. I need cash, fast.'

'Jezuz,' he smirks, 'yer sound like Benny.'

'I wish to meet the owner of Universe.'

He places palms on desk edge, shoves himself back from the desk. 'You mean Richard Sargant? You'll have to lunch Charlie Dimmock.'

'And drink wine?'

'Definitely.'

'Make scintillating conversation?'

'Of course.'

'Desperate times mean desperate measures. Fix it for me, Terry, please.'

He pulls up his trousers, heaves his shoulders to straighten his sports jacket, collects his notes. 'Aye, aye Captain!' He salutes and leaves.

I stride up to my office. Meg is reading a book on Jewish Festivals.

'You'll have to give up bacon butties.'

'Never!' she stuffs the book hastily into her desk drawer.

Tessa and a statuesque woman in a stark black, business suit, exchange a kiss on the cheek. 'Paula how lovely to see you.' Lucinda follows. Two huge melons swing behind a loose scarlet dress.

We're in the bowels of a Soho studio.

'I thought you were terrific on Top of the Pops,' gushes Tessa to Luce, 'I just adore your record. Class act.'

'"The Girl in Tight Pyjamas"? Great, innit? Only got a few words,' Luce simpers.

'Amazing!' Tessa winks at me. She's too good for this job.

'Hi, I'm Ricky.' I shake hands with Paula and Lucinda.

'Now you come with me, Luce.' Tessa leads the doll into the booth. Paula and I sit on upright chairs by Greg the Recording Engineer.

Paula pulls out a contract from her leather attaché case, crosses her legs provocatively. I scan the document.

'We're going to call it Lucinda's Alternative Speaking Clock,' I paraphrase the clauses, 'You'll get £3000 up-front. You get an additional 10% of the money from our revenue. We're only to use your photos in the adverts?'

'That's standard. You have to use at least two,' says Paula.

She hands me five poses: demure, sexy, sophisticated, sucking pencil, dozy.

'I'll take sexy and pencil suck. How much?'

'Five hundred each. I'll invoice you.'

Five Hundred each! 'Ok. I'll sign.' I confirm. It's expensive but could have been worse. Sign a copy and hand it to Paula, who stuffs it an envelope and then tosses it onto the recording desk.

Lucinda dons headphones and sits in a red chair under a huge matching microphone. Tessa pulls up a green chair by her side. Paula stands behind the pair.

I join Greg in his recording lair, surrounded by equipment and separated from them by a one-way glass window.

'You look like a goldfish in there, Tessa,' I shout.

'She can't hear you!' sings Greg. 'Push the button on the mike.'

A red light goes on.

'You look like a goldfish in there, Tess,' I repeat. She scrunches up her face.

'What do *I* look like?' yells Lucinda.

A catfish in subdued light. 'Ravishing!' A wide-eyed Lucinda blushes. Strokes her peroxide blond curls.

'It's unfair, we can't see you.' Tess stares at the plate glass window.

'It's one-way,' whispers Greg. He presses a button, a red light illuminates. 'We start now.'

Lucinda tosses back her long silky mane to turn her brain on. Tess takes Lucinda's hand. 'Now first say the numbers one-to-twelve—slowly.'

'Like this? One... two...' Lucinda responds.

'Great! You're a real pro.' Tessa puts her arm around the back of Lucinda's chair. 'Now one-to-sixty.'

'Cor, you don't ask much, do you?' She counts slowly.

Tessa hands her three sheets of typed paper. 'Now, read through these.'

Lucinda's a startled scared sheep.

Tessa squeezes her arm. 'It's simple, I'll demonstrate. 'Wakey-wakey sleepyheads, you'll be late for work...'

Lucinda pushes the sheets away, 'No-one said I had to read nuffin.' She nibbles her nails.

Paula shoots forward, knocks papers onto the floor. 'Bloody leave your nails alone!'

Lucinda jerks her nails from her mouth.

Paula comes out to join Greg and mutters, 'Stupid cow!'

'*You* never told me she couldn't read Paula.'

She taps my hand with a black designer ballpoint, '*You* never asked, sweetheart. Anyway, 'course she *can* read.'

'Oh yeah? How the hell did she record that song?'

She wags the ballpoint. 'It's only got fifteen words. Anyway, she can read, but she's dyslexic.'

I bang my forehead on the desktop, press the microphone button. 'Tess, say each phrase, then get Luce to repeat it please.' I release the button. 'Can you cope with this, Greg?'

He eyes the second hand on the mammoth wall clock. 'Yeah, but it'll take some time—and editin'.'

'At £300 bloody quid an hour!'

Paula lays her paw on my shoulder. 'Welcome to show-biz, Honey.'

I sit with Terry at a corner table in a trendy, Italian restaurant off Fleet Street. Journos, a handful of MPs, lobbyists, several faces. Gossip and secrets exchanged in whispers, amid the deafening din.

An unkempt, red-faced man tears through the entrance. 'Great to see you, Tel. Bit of a panic back at base. We've caught a Royal in what we call a compromising situation. Had to check with Sarg whether we can publish. Mustn't be too long, right?' He plonks himself down opposite us, reeking of alcohol.

Terry fails to flag down a waiter. 'Fuckin' hell! What do you have to do in this joint to get served?'

I take my mobile from my breast pocket, dial the number displayed on a box of matches.

'Hello, Guiseppe's, can I help you?'

'Do you serve lunch today?'

'*Si, Signor.* Would you like-to-booka-table?'

'I'm at Table 6. I'd like to be served!'

The maitre'd rushes over. 'I so sorry, *signors*. We's so bizzy, I can 'ardly 'ear myself think. Now, what woulda-you-like, eh?'

Terry chokes with laughter into his serviette.

'Mind if I order a glass of plonk?' asks Charlie.

'Let's have a bottle, Charles.' Why not make it six? 'Why don't you choose?'

'That's awfully decent of you.'

An hour later. Terry spies a gorgeous Italian waitress. I kick him, but he gazes dreamily at her. I can see I'll have to deal with Charlie single-handed.

Charlie's mid-anecdote. 'Tel here, says I'll bring Miss World to the Christmas do… and old Tel waltzes in with this Bazilan.' He thumps the table. 'Right shunner she waz. I shay… whatdya see in 'im, love… and she shez… I've never known a man with shutch sexy eyeballs…'

Charlie's in hysterics. Terry only has eyes for Lollobrigida. What time will I get home tonight? Dawn?

Two hours later. They've imbibed three bottles of red. The glass I poured myself at the start is half-full. Charlie's ripe for the kill. His chequered jacket and tie are off. His clammy hand rests on mine as he finishes his seventh drink. Freckled face flushed. Wispy, golden hair is awry.

I look into his baby blue eyes, try the hypnotist's technique I learnt in the East End as a boy. He lurches towards me. Fat face is inches from mine. Can one get sozzled on breath alone? 'Ricky, mate... I wanna to help you... What do I have to do?'

Works every time. Better if they're smashed.

I stare into his soul. 'I wish to meet Richard Sargant. Sarg. Flog him my business.'

Charlie's nods. 'Gimme two weeks. Shumfin' else... we're 'bout to rum a comptission with one of our comptors... win car... Foamworks.... ever 'eard of 'em?'

Phoneworks. Arch enemy. Matt Grabball. Exterminate, Exterminate.

'Yes, yes. Phoneworks. Good company.'

Bastards. Thieves. Liars. 'They're offer-rrrrring eighty pershent poof... hah! Can you hangle... a better deal?'

'We have sufficient lines for calls. As for the deal, would 85 per cent do it?'

'Shounds good...'

He grabs my wrist, holds my watch to his eyes, 'Good heavensh, issh that the time?' He releases me.

I glance at the time. It's 4.30 p.m.

Charlie's tight trousers are about to explode. Sways unsteadily. Table wobbles, bottles set to tumble. Wrestling jacket, waves to Terry who is chatting up Lollobrigida at the bar. Lumbers towards the exit door, staggers outside.

Terry wanders back, thumbs raised. 'Fuckin' Bingo!'

'I have no wish to hear about your geriatric conquests. Beats me what birds see in you.'

'You an' Charlie. I fought you was gonna elope!'

I tug his lapel, 'Now listen, Casanova. I managed to pull off a spectacular business deal while you were AWOL. He's gonna switch a Win-A-Car comp to us from Phoneworks.'

He rests his hand on mine on the table, 'Jezuz, guessed he'd do that. Hates Grabball's guts. Grabball's done the rounds of every department, greasing palms. Problem is, Rick, we're gonna make ourselves an awful lot of enemies. No idea who's on Grabball's pay-roll, but we'll find out soon enough! See yer tomorra.'

As I sign my credit card slip, I see Terry and waitress climb into a taxi.

After a sleepless night, I wait anxiously at my desk for news from Charlie. I reach for my jacket, slung over the guest chair and search each pocket for the Brasserie napkin. Taxi receipts, credit card slips, used Tube tickets. Ah, the napkin with a phone number and the word 'Spells.'

I tap out the number and wait.

'Haa-llo. Spellocity.'

'Hi. You don't know me, I'm a friend of Cosmic Benny.'

'Commie who?'

Perhaps it's a windup? 'Cosmic Benny, Benjamin Kovitz.'

'Oh, Mr Kovitz. Does he call himself Cosmic Benny these days?'

'Benny says you can help,' I reply, avoiding the question.

'Depends.' I doodle an outline of Grabball on the napkin, sticking a pin through its heart.

'You want that man dead?' she asks.

'My god! How did you know?'

'I told her, you idiot,' says God.

'No, no... no that,' Though it's tempting. 'Can you help me sell my business?'

She asks me the name of the business, its address and my birth details then says, 'I think we could help, we'll be in touch in the next few days.'

As I put the phone down, Terry strides through my door, thumbs up. Perky, glowing. immaculate, black blazer, shiny silver buttons.

'Any news?' I ask hopefully.

He opens the Fire Door to create a breeze. 'We've a meeting with the Big Man, Tuesday morning 10 a.m. Mind you're on time.'

I pour myself a sherry from the lone bottle wedged in the bookcase between P.G. Woodhouse and Zola's *La Terre*, collapse in the armchair opposite Susie. She's dolled up in blue kaftan, knitting a garish jumper.

'How was your Mother's group,' I ask.

She ignores my question, 'You spent 2000 quid on spells? Have you completely lost the plot?'

I slurp sherry, wrack my brains for a plausible excuse. We've only gotta couple of grand left before the bailiffs visit, dear, so I thought I'd gamble it on a couple of witches. 'Err, 'fraid, yes.'

She struggles to control her voice, 'Without asking me? Cancel the cheque!'

'I used Amex. The money's gone.'

'Did you consult Mel or Neville or anyone sensible?'

'Benny...'

She howls. 'That crack-head?'

'He's sober, reformed now.'

She shakes her head sadly, 'You'll be asking Seth next.'

'I'm sorry, darling. It won't happen again. I promise.'

We sit silently. God whispers, 'Remember the Offering. The one bought for many shekels.'

Oh, the present. 'I nearly forgot!' I exclaim. I run to the hall, extract a gift-wrapped package from my pocket. I bow as I hand it to her. 'For you, sweetheart.'

She unwraps it, frowns. 'A perfume bottle! How many thousands did this cost?' Then relents, pulls me to her, plants a kiss on my cheek. 'You're mad, Rickele, but I love you.'

I dread Sonny's prophecy, 'You, your wife, your beautiful baby, homeless in fog and snow.'

17

I enter Sargant House in Chancery Lane. It's an uninspiring 60s block. A security guard orders me to sign in, copies my name onto a badge.

'Wear this, please, Sir.'

My big chance has arrived – my opportunity to sell Ring-Inn, pay off bloody loan sharks, be free!

An oak-panelled mirrored lift whisks me to the fourth floor. I check my tie for kinks, lips for marmalade, pin the badge to my lapel. Outside the lift, an anxious Charlie greets me. He peers into the empty lift as I scan Reception.

'Where's Tel?' he asks.

'Fuck!' we say in unison.

Tel's usually Mr Punctual. Only a nuclear explosion would make him late. I look outside the window for bomb damage.

'He'll be here soon.' I reply hopefully.

Charlie's an unhappy bunny. 'Blast and bugger him!'

Two receptionists with name tags sit on a raised platform by gigantic oak doors. Official entrance to the inner sanctum?

'Mr Tomblin?' asks Dee.

'Ricky Stern.' I point to my name. She cranes her head forward to inspect my official badge.

'Mr Sargant insists Mr Tomblin is present. Let's have your coat.' She hangs it in a cupboard. 'Luckily, Mr Sargant's running late. If Mr Tomblin's not here by 10.25 a.m. we'll have to abort the meeting.'

Charlie scowls. 'Never get another chance.'

We pace the room. Is Terry playing a devious game? Throttle him.

Neon clocks display the correct time in New York, Warsaw, London. 10.15 a.m. here. I eye a small door behind Dee. Tradesmen's entrance into Sarg? Ceiling camera trained on me. Black and white-tiled marble floor displays circular initial "S". My heart beats wildly. I flick through the Sargant Communications Annual Report. On the first page, Sarg proudly announces: 'Our competent team are building a fine global communications business together.'

A courier arrives. 'Take this to the Russian Embassy, make sure you get a legible signature,' says Sherry.

Her intercom barks an order, 'Drop *this* one at number 10.' She pushes the button.

'Yes, Sarg. Right away.'

She pops through the small door, emerges with a new package, hands it to the messenger. As he leaves, he collides with Terry.

'I've just delivered a baby on the District Line,' he shouts as he swans over to us.

Baloney!

'You must be Mr Tomblin,' says Sherry.

He waltzes up to the two pretty assistants. 'That I am. Two attractive ladies, if ever I saw 'em.' They titter. 'Now my darlings, you can tell your Sarg we're ready for him.' He winks as he hands them his Burberry raincoat.

'I'm late for an editorial meeting,' says Charlie. 'Good luck!' He presses a button and the vast lift swallows him up.

'Mr Sargant will see you now.' Gigantic doors slide open. 'Go through, please.'

We walk several feet and the second pair of doors swing open.

A Yeti extends a hairy paw. 'Come in, gentlemen. Richard Sargant!' he booms. He towers above us in a creased white shirt, kipper tie with a polar bear motif. Enormous puffy face, thick eyebrows, brown wavy hair.

'I'm a fan of yours, Mr Tomblin. Follow all your tips. Won over a grand last week.' He peers down at me. 'And *you* are?' Never met such a huge man before, he'd crush me with one foot. 'Ricky Stern,' I mutter. He grinds my hand in his paw, lifts me off the carpet.

'Welcome to my lair, Boys.'

An Aladdin's cave. Exotic, ornately carved, oak desk. Six multi-coloured telephones. Intercom. Two giant chairs. Music videos project on far wall.

'My new music channel. We'll put MTV out of business!' He points to a large Alpine horn which takes pride of place on a zebra skin. 'Gift from the Bank of Switzerland. I borrowed money from them.'

'HSBC only gave me a piggy bank,' I say.

'Change banks then.' His chest heaves with laughter. One puff and he'll blow the house down.

He drags over a guest chair, clambers unsteadily onto it. Purses his lips, blows on the horn. His body quivers, cheeks turn purple. Gasps of a dying whale. Chair creaks in tune. He descends to the floor again, precariously.

A uniformed butler enters through the tradesmen's door carrying a silver tray with china cups and a teapot.

He places the tray on the desk, offers Sarg a huge mug of tea. Two cups of tea for us.

'I hear you're a quasi-religious man, Stern. Come with me.' He leads Tel and me to a pile of ancient books in a corner. 'This Talmud was owned by Henry VIII.'

'Talmood?' Terry strokes it.

'Tell him.' Sarg nods at me.

'A Jewish commentary,' I explain.

'You've read my autobiography?' continues Sarg.

'No, I am sorry.' I don't lie in case he asks questions. Are we ever going to get on with it? I have a business to sell.

He picks up two autobiographies from a stack. 'Here you go, let me know what you think of it.' He hands copies to us both.

The inside cover reads, 'Best wishes from Richard Sargant.'

'Dee signed 'em,' he chuckles. 'You'll see I started from nothing. My name back then was unpronounceable, so I changed it. These were my parents.' He points at a framed image of two doting peasants on the back cover. 'I fled the Nazis, made a new life. British army refused to enlist me. Called myself Sargant, couldn't spell. Now I speak 15 languages, own successful companies in 50 countries.'

The distorted intercom announces, 'Russian Ambassador.'

Sargant returns to his desk, lifts a red phone. Talks animatedly in Russian. We climb onto the high guest seats to sip tea. My legs dangle in mid-air.

Sargant replaces the receiver. 'So, Mr Tomblin, what can I do for you?'

'Call me Terry, please. Rick here has a phone business, don't you Rick?'

Nerves prevent me speaking. 'Yes,' I croak. Fuck, fuck, fuck.

'Tell me 'bout it,' invites Sarg.

I strain my vocal cords. 'Premium lines.' Holy Moses, I'm a castrated chipmunk!

'What was that?' asks Sarg.

'Water,' I point at my throat.

'Ah!' He presses his intercom. 'Dee, send in water. My young guest is choking to death.'

Terry leaps to my rescue. 'Premium lines. We're the largest in the UK. We cover Sport, Horoscopes, Finance. We're seeking a partnership with Sargant Communications.'

Sarg leans forward, fist on the table, hairy eyebrow raised. 'Partnership or fuck-off cash?'

'We're open to any reasonable deal.'

Sarg's fist closes. 'Unfortunately, you may be too late, gentlemen. We're already using Phoneworks... met their CEO yesterday.' He presses his intercom button, 'Who was the guy I met yesterday, honey – with Hopkins?'

'Mr Grabball, Sarg,' replies Dee.

Annihilate! Exterminate! Should be grateful for such a tenacious rival, but I'd like to cut his throat.

'You wouldn't want to work with them,' warns Terry.

'And why not?' asks Sarg.

'They're dishonest bastards.'

Ah!' Sarg seems pleased as he opens a worn, leather daybook, jots with a Parker pen. 'Dimcock speaks highly of your organisation. Wants to run a promotion with you.' Twiddles pen. 'Grabball told me you couldn't cope with the excessive calls. That true?'

Dee pops in, hands me a paper cup. I gulp down iced water. 'Rubbish!' I exclaim, vocal at last.

'Thought you might say that, but I'm prepared to take the risk. Charlie has a soft spot for Terry here.' Makes another jot, 'Tell me, Terry, precisely what happened on the District Line?'

'You should've fuckin' been there.'

'I've a chauffeur,' retorts a jovial Sarg.

'This woman, musta bin nine months' preggers, starts screamin' she's havin' a kid. I knew what to do 'cos I worked on a farm. I pull Emergency. The train grinds to a stop at Ken High. I use me jacket as a pillow, Evian water to daub her brow. Clear a space on the platform. Within minutes, the baby pops out. Used my Swiss Army knife to cut the cord.'

'Well done!' says Sarg. Tel's a fibber.

He picks up a green phone. 'Dim-cock? Great story. Universe Man Delivers Infant on District Line.' Sarg puts Charlie on speakerphone.

'Sarg, Tel doesn't work for us,' replies Charlie.

'Does now, he'll be our Special Correspondent.'

'Travel or Racing?' asks Charlie.

'Both.' Shouts into the receiver, 'Fix it, right?' Turns to us. 'Now, gentlemen, if that'll be all, I have a lunch appointment with the Israeli Ambassador.'

'One last thing,' interjects Terry.

'And what would that be?' asks Sarg.

'Someone's fobbed you off with a fake Talmud, unless you nicked it from the British Library.'

'Strange things happen in life,' twinkles Sarg.

Two sets of doors slide open. We leap off our perches, shake hands, leave. Dee hands us our coats.

In the lift, I say, 'That was a disaster, a complete and utter shambles. First, you turn up late, then I lose my bloody voice.'

Terry squeezes my arm. 'You could apply for a part in a Disney cartoon. Come, let's wind up Hopkins.'

'You crazy?' Why not throw ourselves off a cliff face?

'Look, Sunshine, we got the promotion, right?'

The lift halts at the 3rd floor. We cross an enclosed walkway to Sargant Tower. Another lift transports us to Editorial on the 8th. A sea of screens greets us with journos typing frenetically.

Hopkins scowls as we approach. 'I know your little game!' He stands in his doorway, arms akimbo. His rolled-up shirtsleeves reveal tanned arms.

'Let me make myself abundantly clear. We're perfectly happy with Phoneworks. I'll run a promotion with you, 'cos I've had my arm twisted by Sarg plus our illustrious editor. But, if there's the slightest hiccup, I'll pull the comp from you bastards and switch it to Phoneworks. Now, fuck off!'

'Putty in our hands,' says Terry, as we walk to the lifts watched by Hopkins and his bemused editorial team.

In dawn light, I wander down West End Lane to Mistry Newsagents. I smell the incense from his morning *puja*. Newspapers lie in neat piles on the floor. Mr Mistry counts each one.

I find a copy of Universe, *Win-a-Mini: Phone Entry*, hold it up to Mr Mistry. 'Can I buy this?'

He's bent over Telegraphs. 'I counting. Minute please. Now, what you are wantin'?'

'Universe, please.'

He cuts a plastic ribbon with a penknife, stares at Win a Mini: Phone Entry, hands it over with ink-stained fingers. 'That's my competition.'

He looks surprised.

'You in motor business?'

'I handle phone calls.' I point to Phone Entry.

'*That* is business?' he says as I hand him 20p.

I drive to the office car park at 8 a.m. As I lock my car door, I hear a tin can rattle. A guy runs through the gates and disappears. Probably a homeless soul.

I climb the entrance steps and peer into Reception.

Des has his back to me. He wears large silver headphones. His body sways rhythmically. He grasps two rulers and drums the desk. I ring the night bell, but he's oblivious.

I dial the office number on my mobile. One ring, white light on the switchboard blinks. He doesn't notice. Five rings, all the phones in the building echo in unison. Des's deaf. Ten rings, red light over his desk flashes. Contact. Des hurls the drumsticks onto the desk, pulls off the headphones, and picks up the switchboard phone.

'H-hello? Ring-Inn.'

'Des?'

'Who's that? That you, Sean?' He swings round and sees me staring through the glass door. 'Look, Sean. Can't talk now, Guvnor's turned up.'

'It's not Sean, it's me, it's Ricky. On my mobile.'

'Fuck!'

He attempts to rise, gets caught up in wire from headphones. Untangles himself, lumbers to the door. Blue woollen jersey, stolen from prison, unzipped jeans, trainers. Dishevelled hair.

'Sorry, Guv.'

I point to his flies. 'Oops!' He uses his index finger to zip up. Wipes his hand on a sweaty jumper. 'Guv, I've bought you a Christmas present.' He searches his hold-all, extracts an LP. Young Des and three Desettes stand backs to the wall.

I must gauge how the promotion's going!

'Oh, Des, very kind.' Tobacco stench. 'It's an album we made before I went...' tear forms in his right eye. 'Will you listen to it?'

For fuck's sake.

God, 'I have created every Creature! All serve My Purpose.'

Des produces a battered tape recorder, thumps it on the desktop, switches it on. Pleasant sound, like the Eagles.

'Rather good, Des... but have to dash.' I tear through to our machine room, run to the display screen. Not a single light. Pick up the wall-phone, dial the competition number. Engaged! Replace the receiver, bang my head on the computer, howl – why me?

'Trust in the Almighty and the Truth shall be revealed unto you.'

I ring Gary's number. Luckily, he has just arrived. 'We have a major disaster on our hands. Can you come immediately?'

Gary rushes into the computer room, toolbox in hand. Quietly confident. Slips behind the computer, unlocks a flap, pokes around with a metal prong and gauge.

'Problem's outside. I'll check the junction box.' Strides out into the forecourt.

Des turns off his tape, 'Summat wrong, Guv?'

'Satan's declared war,' I shout.

'Anything I can do?'

'Pray.'

Gary examines a cabinet by the front gate, 'Cable's severed. We'll need Telecom.'

Sabotage! Must have been that guy rushing out of the carpark.

That bastard Grabball. 'How long before it's fixed, Gary?'

He scratches his head, 'We have a 24/7 maintenance contract. Hopefully before lunch. Latest early afternoon.'

I leave Gary fiddling, return to Reception.

'Call for you, Guv,' Des hands me phone.

Croaky voice says, 'Ricky? Charlie Dimmock.'

'Hi, Charles.'

'Rick, everythin' workin'?'

Matt bloody Grabball paid a rogue Telecom stooge to cut the main cable, render the computer powerless, screw up our once-in-a-lifetime opportunity to handle a Universe promotion.

'Of course,' I reply.

He pauses. 'Only, I've rung the number ten times. Always get engaged.'

'I'll check it out. Tel will ring you back.'

Gary passes me. 'Telecom on their way. I'll run checks in the machine room. Nothing more I can do 'til they arrive.'

I stagger into the main office, collapse in a chair. Dapper Terry's next to arrive, clutching a champagne bottle. Dumps it down, 'This is a great fuckin' day!'

'Glad you think so,' I say.

'Jezuz, what's it take to cheer you up?'

'We've been sabotaged.'

'Sabotaged?'

'Some bastard's cut the Telecom cable from our computer to the outside world.'

He folds his arms, 'Jezuz fuckin' Christ' Mouth drops open.

Tessa breezes in, 'Exciting Day!'

'Tell her, Terry. I don't have the strength.' Terry whispers in her ear.

'Oh no!' she replies and hugs me.

'I'm off to talk tactics with Terry in his office,' I say. If anyone calls from Universe, take a message. Haven't told them there's a problem yet, so don't let on.'

Terry's office is partitioned off at one end of the first floor. Hangs his jacket on a hanger on a metal coat-stand. Sits behind a bare black desk under shots of sleek greyhounds.

'You'd better hope Glen Hopkins hasn't got news of this cock-up.' Says Terry glumly.

I lean on the white brick wall to face him. 'Charlie rang 30 mins ago. Couldn't get through to the Comp. If Charlie knows, I reckon that bastard Glen will be calling at any moment.'

He swings his hand towards me. 'And folks here?'

'Only Gary and Tessa.'

'When will it be fixed?'

'Lunchtime, if we're lucky.'

'Let me talk to Charlie. You cheer up the troops.'

I leave his room and slump by Tessa, who says, 'You look ghastly, sweetheart. Like a cup of peppermint tea?'

'Thanks. And plain tea for Tel.'

Gary screams, 'Rick? Meg's got Glen Hopkins on the line.'

Here's my Waterloo, my Dunkirk, my Armageddon. 'Put him through!'

Hopkins shouts, 'I've two words for you. You're fired! You bastards couldn't organise your way out of a paper bag. I'm goin' to Sarg. We're switchin' to Phoneworks from tomorrow. And you can forget any ideas you had about sellin' to us. 'Bye, loser.'

'It's over,' I say to Terry.

'Charlie can't help us. Hopkins has been badmouthing us saying there's a fault.'

I crawl under the desk, curl up in a foetal position, suck my thumb. Tessa kneels, 'Let me take you away from all this, darling?'

'A woman from something called Spellocity on the line? You don't want it, Rick, do you? Shall I tell her to piss off?' Gary covers the mouthpiece.

I grab the phone 'Hello!' I scream loudly.

'Hi, how is it going Mr Stern?' she asks.

'My computer's sabotaged, my main client's fired me and destroyed my business.'

'So, something is happening?!'

'Hardly the result I needed.'

'It's early days. Sometimes it's necessary to go backwards before going forwards.' She answers enigmatically. I bid her farewell.

I'll get Benny to reimburse me. Spellocity was his rotten idea. Oh, he's broke. How could I forget?

Tessa shouts. 'Jake Jones, Randolph Communications is on the phone.'

'Randolph? Remind me?' I ask Terry.

'Humungous Yankee media outfit. Owner Brad Randolph. Bought National Sentinel.'

That's strange. They're Universe's main competitor. Oh, God, we do their racing services! He'll be complaining he can't dial them. 'Transfer him to this phone, Tess.' I pick up the receiver. 'Hi Jake, Rick speaking.'

High voice with a Welsh lilt says, 'Ricky, we've never met, but I know all about you. OK to talk?'

'Fire away,' I reply trying to sound nonchalant.

'Randolph wants to diversify internationally into Telecoms. They've asked me to suggest high-growth European targets. We did a search and your company came up. Your turnover's tiny, but your growth rate and profits are exceptional. I'd like to meet. Interested?'

'That would be great.' Maybe Spellocity aren't crap after all.

'Be at the Stafford Hotel, St. James, 3 p.m. tomorrow.'

I hurl the receiver onto its cradle.

'Well?' ask Gary, Terry and Tessa.

I toast them with champagne. 'May I take this opportunity to recommend spells and witches.'

The lounge of the Stafford's comfortable, old-fashioned place. Woodfire crackles in the grate. Lift transports me to the fourth floor. The door of room 403 is ajar. I knock.

A distant voice shouts 'Come!..' I enter nervously.

'Take a pew.' Jake beckons me to an armchair, he lounges on a sofa. Beige woollen suit. Balding grey hair, thin face, elfin ears. Produces small notepad, fiddles with a propelling pencil.

'Aberystwyth's a grim place,' remarks Jake, for no apparent reason.

'Couldn't wait to escape. Blagged my way onto a cargo ship. Woke up stoned under the Statue of Liberty. Got a job in Sidewalks ad sales, worked my way up, bought by Brad, stuck with him ever since. My job's to think.'

What shall I say? Computer programmer, forged CBE, jettisoned from an international software company, house mortgaged up to hilt, wife and child to support, about to be thrown out by bailiffs.

I continue in full bullshit mode. 'I'm... building a telecoms company. I've identified a unique opening. Premium Calls – but that's only for starters. With your newspapers,' and my genius, 'we could develop a competitor to old Telecom.'

Jake stares at me in silence for what seems an age, 'Ricky, it's been a pleasure. You're our sort of guy, one of us. Give me your numbers.'

'That's it Jake? All you need to know?'

'I know the sort of guy Brad needs. I've been talent spotting for him for years. He holds out his hand as I retrieve a creased business card from my pocket. He stuffs it into his bulging wallet. 'I'll talk it over with Brad. Be a few days. Brad's based in New York. You'll need to meet him there. That OK?'

'Sure. Love New York.' I mutter. Bloody Hell!

18

I keep worrying about Grabball. He sabotaged our Universe competition. He'd stop at nothing.

I call Terry for a chinwag. He arrives flushed and flustered without his blazer.

'Fuckin' incompetents! They put Newmarket results on the Cheltenham line. Lucky, I spotted it.' He sways from foot to foot in my open office doorway.

'If it's inconvenient...' I repond.

'No.' His brow furrows.

'Please sit, you make me nervous.' I point at the sofa.

He crouches on the edge of my black leather sofa. Beside him sits a weeping fig with variegated leaves and sticker, “Supplied by Green Fingers”.

‘Terry, I’m worried about Grabball. He sabotaged our competition. Maybe he’s bugging us...’

Terry glances round the room warily, crouches onto all fours to peer under my desk, then backs out. ‘You’re fuckin’ paranoid, no taps here, clean as a whistle.’ He lifts my phone, peers underneath, prowls round my office poking and prodding. Then he grabs writing pen and pad and scrawls: *Don’t say a word, meet Café Delancey, five mins.* ‘I’d best be off, work piling up.’ He winks as he slopes away.

I don my raincoat and waterproof cap, dash down the fire escape, head through drizzle to Delanceys. No sign of him at crowded front tables. I head past the cluttered bar with its large green cups stacked on a coffee machine and find Terry in a back alcove. Sits by roaring fire in a bare-bricked room. Table set for four, red rose, green-checked linen cloth, smell of burning wood.

He chats up a red-head with a ponytail. Silver bangles, red clogs, blue and white apron. She stands, hand on his heart-shaped chair back, giggling. He pats her behind. ‘Off you go, my darlin’, me boss has arrived!’

‘You want sumfink to drink?’ she asks in Slovakaise.

‘What you having, Tel?’

He glances at the menu through thick specs. 'Irish Coffee.'

'Make that two.' I add.

She throws him a seductive smile, smirks at me, flounces off.

Tel leans towards me to whisper. I can't hear him above a crooner singing "Stormy Weather". 'Your whole joint is fuckin' wired,' he hisses.

'Not so loud!' I glance around the empty room. 'How do you know?'

Commander Stern, secret agent on dangerous assignation.

'How else does fuckin' Grabball know what colour pants I'm wearing?' says Tel.

'Maybe he asked the waitress.' I reply.

'Jezuz, Rick. It's no laughing matter.' His lower lip trembles, face cracks mouth howls with laughter.

The waitress returns with two steaming drinks, 'You boyz certainly know how to have a good time.' She serves, waltzes off.

Terry leers then regains his composure. 'I'll give you Leonard Turnball's number... call him from a phone box... Cheers!' He slurps, licks white chocolate from his lips with a circular motion of his fat tongue.

Bulldog Private Detective Leonard Turnball ploughs into full English brekkers at a local cafe, surrounded by builders, electricians and handymen. Roasts in his trench coat in the steamy room. The smell of fried bacon, Finchley Road petrol fumes. Tells me he works from home, delighted to escape his wife and kids.

Waves his knife in my direction, mouth full of egg yolk.

'So, what makes you think you're bugged?' Leonard asks me.

I wait for a lorry to pass. 'The fact our main competitor knew about our launch party, a promotion with a national newspaper, everything actually.' He concentrates on his bacon as if he hadn't eaten for months.

'Any disgruntled employees?'

Gary wants a rise, Basil promotion, Tessa hates me, Des hates his uniform. 'No, not really.'

'Hmm!' He cuts and demolishes a slice of fat-rind. 'I could run a wire detector round your place. If we find taps, we leave'em, hide a camera. After a couple of days, we catch the bugger. I doubt the perpetrator would use wireless. More likely, we'll find hidden recorders. Tapes would be replaced regularly. Must be someone who has unchallenged access.'

'The plant people, Green Fingers?'

'Brace yourself. It's usually someone who's been working closely with you. The person you'd least suspect.'

Meg? Tessa? 'When can we do it? How much?'

He extracts a diary and bitten pencil from a crumpled jacket pocket, flicks through it. 'How 'bout tonight.' He looks up cross-eyed. 'The bug sweep's £500, rental of a camera £200, then there's my time. Call it a grand.'

'You're on.'

He glances around the room, rises, dons his raincoat. Places a heavy hand on my shoulder. 'And don't tell a bloody soul, for God's sake!'

Des eyes me anxiously. It's late evening, he wants to sneak off to the computer room for a kip. Moth-eaten sleeping bag stuffed under the desk.

'You expecting someone, Guv?'

He wears prison chic. Brown ribbed jersey, dirty grey woollen tracksuit bottoms, lank dishevelled hair.

'A Telecom engineer is coming in to do some tests.'

'Telecom? At this time of night?' He rolls his eyes heavenwards.

A van pulls into the forecourt. A burly Turnball in a corporate boiler suit descends. I rush out into the chilly air to greet him.

'Where did you get the van and clobber?'

'Connections,' he replies. Connections, Telecom. Very funny. 'Where's the junction box?' The moon lights up his pockmarked face.

'Over there by the bins, behind the flower barrel.'

I lead him across the courtyard. He carries a large toolbox, torch. Unlocks the box, rummages around. I crouch beside him, peer into the cabinet. Heady smell of wilting flowers, garbage.

'Here's the beauty.' He shines his torch on a small black recorder. 'Hooked to one line only. You have a direct line?'

'Yeah.'

'I'll wager it's tapped.'

Recognition, at last. 'Can you disable it?'

'What? Advertise we're on 'is tail?' Commander Stern, buffoon.

A distant voice shouts, 'Everythin' all right, Guv?'

'Who the fuck's that?' asks Turnball.

'Our Night Guard.'

He chucks tools frantically back into his van. 'Distract 'im while I close the cabinet.'

A ghoulish Des rises up, illuminated by floodlight. Unlaced plimsolls. 'What's up Guv?'

'Engineer's checking a fault.'

Des peers over my shoulder, suspicious. 'Go inside, Des.'

'Don't say that, Guv. That word... inside... gives me the heebie-geebies.'

'Sorry, Des, but go!'

'Okey-dokey,' He shuffles in through the entrance, glancing back.

Turnball materialises by my side. 'Let's check the building.'

We go to the reception entrance. Des lays down *Asian Babes*, buzzes us in.

Out of his hearing, Turnball says, 'First we'll check your office.'

As I escort him, he whispers, 'Don't say anything 'til I've run a full sweep. OK?'

He extracts a meter and metal probe from his toolbox, paces the room. Meter swings wildly at a rubber plant. He snorts, removes topsoil with expert fingers, extracts recorder, replaces it. Then he inspects the whole room, points to the silver ducting tube which runs round the wall above the desk. Pulls out a small camera, a black metallic box, clambers onto the desk, fixes them with the camera pointing at the pot. Beckons me downstairs.

As we exit to the forecourt, Des calls, 'Make sure you get the van back by midnight!'

'Cheeky devil.' I say, 'Des is on to us.'

'Can you trust him?' asks Turnball.

'Des? Needs the lolly.'

'Didn't give off the right vibe. Too cocksure. But you were right about the plant company. I suspect they've been paid a couple of hundred quid to keep *schtum*, but it still needs an insider to change tapes. See you Thursday evening.'

Turnball opens the van's back door, slings his toolbox onto the floor, slams the door shut, revs engine, drives off.

Terry sits by the Delancey bar, facing the roadside window. Above is a sketch of a man's foot, multi-coloured socks, playing footsie with the mistress. 'Progress on Wedlock. Turnball thinks we have a mole,' I say.

'Wedlock?' asks a baffled Tel. He chomps French bread, sips filter coffee.

'Codeword for covert operation.'

Tips back chair, 'Who thought up that fuckin' stupid name?'

I slurp tea, 'You said wedlock was the last thing you'd ever consider!'

'Fuckin' crazy!' About to lose balance, jerks forward, rights chair, whispers, 'I know who the mole is... It's gotta be Gary. Why else did he keep that rocket?'

'Or Baz, or Des, or... You!'

He guffaws. 'I'm no undercover agent!' Eyes blonde with green highlights who slinks by, biro stuck into stray locks.

'This time tomorrow, we'll know the worst.'

'More technical probs?' asks Des. Plays Battleships on an old PC the company donated for him to practise computer literacy. Chats online when I'm not around, masterminding counter-espionage missions.

'Just routine checks,' I explain.

He smirks and clicks away.

Telecom van roars up to entrance steps. Turnball, in Telecom guise, dashes into Reception.

'Have you come to check the junction box?' asks an inquisitive Des.

A haggard Turnball slams the door shut, shouts, 'Why don't you mind your own bloody business?' Boiler suit's a size too small. Snake's head pops out of tight collar. Swollen veins.

I grab his arm. 'Let's go to the machine-room.'

Once in my office, Turnball says, 'It's been a long day, I can do without smart alec's.'

He clambers onto the desk, dismantles the camera and recorder from a metal air-conditioning conduit, hands them to me. I lay them on the carpet, steady him as he climbs down.

'Does that work?' He points at my video player, by the Fire Exit.

'Sure.' He ejects the tape from the recorder. I place it in the machine.

We watch fast-forward, as the previous night's events appear on the screen. Long-distance loneliness of humble weeping fig. Suddenly, the fig tree is bathed in light. Man's figure jerkily pokes earth.

'Hey-ho! *Cherchez la Femme*.' Turnball's triumphant.

I stop the tape, rewind for thirty seconds, set Play at normal speed.

'Who's the blighter?' asks Turnball.

I can't make the head out. Then the handsome features, natty dress, give the game away.

'Gavin Penhaligon, our landlord.' I gasp. The Bastard!

I instruct Turnball to sweep the whole building. No further taps. I confiscate the plant recorder. He disconnects the junction box and drives away. Gavin's Land Rover's parked outside his office. Too late to disturb him.

After a sleepless night, I stand outside his door, buzz.

'It's not feeding time, Des. Piss off!'

'It's me, Ricky. Can we talk?'

'At 7.30, blimey! Can't it wait?' There's a sweet scent from the flower box by the door.

'It's urgent.'

'Oh... just a tic.'

The door buzzes. I head up narrow, wooden stairs. Gavin sits at a desk, slurps cornflakes from a large white ceramic bowl and coffee from a mug. Large windows open inwards, revealing a panoramic view of the canal. Chilly wind rustles charcoal life drawings pinned to the wall.

He wears dark suit trousers, a pink open-necked business shirt, gleaming black shoes. Fresh, newly-showered, damp hair swept back. Expensive after-shave. The door behind him leads to the bed and bath-room.

'Coffee?' he indicates a hot tray, percolator on top of the fridge. 'Help yourself.' I pour coffee into a clean mug, dash of milk from a matching jug.

'Why the dawn visitation?' He munches away.

'Gavin, why are you bugging me?'

'You haven't run out of toilet rolls again? Can't your staff crap at home?'

'Your tape recorder's hidden in my office plant.'

'What?' Bleery eyes peer at me.

Someone moving next door. 'You gotta guest?' I ask.

He raises his eyebrows. 'So?'

'I found a video of you replacing tape in the record-er.'

'Is there a law against it?'

'Gavin, it's an offence to bug my office.'

'What a scandalous accusation. Repeat it. I'll sue.'

'I have the tape.' I emphasise.

'I've got a commercial arrangement with Green Fingers. They kit out the place free with plants, I refresh tapes on a daily basis, they make a generous donation to the Shropshire Hunt.'

'Bugging my room?'

'That's absolutely no concern of mine.'

'And the tap in the courtyard Telecom box?'

'News to me, you're in that business.' A smug Gavin leans back, splash of milk on chin.

'Gavin, allow me to let you into a little secret which you probably already know. We're about to be acquired by Randolph Corporation. If they discover, you're colluding with the enemy, they'll come after you with a vengeance.'

He ponders. 'If I kick out Green Fingers, you'll have to compensate me.'

'How much?'

He licks lips. 'Five grand.'

'Five bleedin' grand?'

'Take it or leave it. What's it to you when you'll make squillions?'

I weigh up the pros and cons. Legal wrangle's the last thing I need during the acquisition. Five grand'll keep Gavin off the case while the deal goes through.

'Okay, Okay,' I sigh.

'Cheque by noon, they'll be out by five,' he grimaces.

'Yes, yes.' I rise to leave.

'One more thing,' he insists. 'Yesterday you had five cars in the car park—again. Know your lease allows only three. From now on, I'm fining you £1,000 for the first transgression, doubling it each subsequent time.'

'You can't do that!'

'Watch me!' Turns to window to watch gates open as water sluices into the murky Lock.

19

Jake from Randolph Communications called at 7 a.m. Had given up on him. It's been 10 days. Brad Randolph has summoned me to meet him in New York tomorrow afternoon! Ring Continental Airlines. Book a flight.

Terminal 3 Heathrow. Refuge for asylum seekers. Arabs in turbans, bright African robes, Indian *dhotis*, backpackers, failed entrepreneurs. A barrage of unintelligible announcements bombard from the Tannoy. I make out 'delayed', 'cancelled' and 'apologise.'

I pick my way over bodies in sleeping bags, towards Continental check-in. No queue. A red-headed check-in girl in a black uniform thrusts a form across the counter.

'Sign this please, Sir. It's a waiver form.' Her eyes are cold.

She turns it sideways, 'There are blizzards in New York. Basically, it's in case we're diverted. So you can't sue.'

'And if I won't sign?

'Then you can't board, Sir.'

I love girls in uniform.

I dash down gangway. She blocks my way onto plane. I kiss her neck, she drags me into an empty cockpit.

I sign the form.

I settle back in my seat. Endure *Driving Miss Daisy* on the overhead screen, force down lasagne, gulp a glass of red wine, fail to chat up the frail damsel beside me who grasps the armrests.

Mighty Brad grabs my hand. 'Gee Ricky, I'm so honoured to meet you.' Commander Stern bows. 'It's a pleasure, Brad.'

Suddenly the movie freezes, Captain's voice informs us we're diverting to Chicago!

Susie's tucked up at home, while I *schlep* round the globe at 31,000 feet. Knackered Commander Stern, lone fighter. Why aren't I in a regular job? *Schlemiel!* I'm en-route to a second-class Chicago motel. Maybe Grabball's piloting the plane.

Flash of lightning sears past reinforced glass windows, plane buffets. I catch my carton of orange juice before it slides off my tray.

God says, 'Repent ye sinners!'

I stagger into the arrivals' hall, clutching my Gladstone bag. Frantic travellers queue for pay phones, shout at airline staff and each other. 'Get outta my way, mister!' A porter barges into me with his trolley.

I find a quiet corner, dump my bag on the floor. Close my eyes.

'Ricky Stern, aren't you Ricky Stern?' asks a fat travelling salesman, in a creased suit. 'Say, you don't remember me, do you? Chop!' He lowers his hand for a shake.

It can't be. Don Smith. Shakes my hand vigorously.

A sign. Wait a minute. Can this really be just a coincidence?

'What you doing here Don?'

'Oh, you know?' he answers vaguely.

'Anyway, I'm going to miss my New York meeting. Just want to go home now.'

'Suggest you talk to Sandy over there.' He points to a young fella at the Continental Desk. 'Just tell him Don sent you. Chop!' He shakes my hand, almost pulling fingers from their sockets. He looks at his watch. Shoots off.

I approach chirpy Sandy at the Continental Desk. 'I'd like to go home,' I beg.

He eyes me sympathetically. 'Where's home, sir?'

'London, England.'

He pats my elbow. 'We don't fly direct from Chicago, Sir. You'll have to take our flight to New York tomorrow morning in order to connect.'

'Is there any way I can get back to London tonight?'

His eyes harden, 'I am sorry, Sir.'

'Umm, Don sent me.'

He looks surprised, whispers furtively in my ear, 'Go to gate C7 at 5 p.m. If anyone asks, say Sandy sent you.'

Commander Stern stumbles towards the Gate to Salvation, where an unscheduled plane will repatriate him. His mission is in tatters. The most powerful man in the world – Brad Randolph – is bottled by a penniless, software salesman. Two hundred nicker down the pan.

Famished, I buy a cheese sandwich and orange juice, carry them to the deserted gate. Outside a snow blizzard rages.

I call Susie from a pay phone. 'Hello, darling.'

'Are you in New York?'

I sound matter-of-fact. 'Plane diverted to Chicago. Hopefully, I'll hitch a ride home tonight on a 747.'

'But sweetheart, what about the Brad Megabucks meeting?'

'No way I can make it to New York before the weekend. I'll ring his office when I get back. It's nighttime now.'

Homeless in fog and snow.

'I'm sure it'll all work out.'

'Night-night, darling. See you tomorrow.'

A young nerd with a backpack approaches me. He checks me out to see if I'm trustworthy. I munch my sandwich. He whispers, 'Sandy sent me,' and slumps into a blue, plastic bucket seat next to mine.

'How did you wangle that?' I ask.

He retrieves a banana from his Anorak. 'He's dating my cousin.' He unzips banana, munches.

Eventually, we are six males. Six musketeers. Sandy jogs towards us. God's AWOL but at least Sandy's here. 'We are flying the crew back to London. Should be ready to board at 7 p.m.'

Can't believe it. My very own 747. Paid £199 for an Atlantic joy ride.

By Friday lunchtime, 9 a.m. New York time, I'm back at my Camden desk calling Brad's office. Amazingly his secretary apologises to me.

'I couldn't reach you on Thursday to save you the trip. Brad's stuck in Chicago. Weather's atrocious. He wonders if you could come over on Concorde Monday morning to meet him in New York. As our guest, naturally.'

Brad was in fucking Chicago too! Ye Gods.

'Watch your language,' he bellows.

'Let me check my diary for Monday.' I have a gig with my dentist. Suppose I could reschedule. 'I'd be delighted.' Concorde, huh? *Fly me to the moon and let me play among the stars...*

'The ticket will be waiting for you at Check-in. Just come right along to our offices at noon-thirty.'

At Heathrow, I pick up my Concorde ticket from the British Airways desk. The return is the next day overnight in Business. Cheapskates!

Check-in and then admire the plane from the waiting area. Beautiful. Looking forward to my once-in-a-lifetime luxurious ride. But as I enter the passenger area, the fantasy disintegrates. It resembles a bus! In fact, I have to keep reminding myself this is a supersonic plane. No TV either just a screen with our speed (currently zero!). Luckily, I bought a copy of *Tinker, Tailor, Soldier, Spy* in Departures. That will keep me occupied.

I'm crammed next to a guy absorbed in a script. I'm in the window seat, so he rather begrudgingly stands up and allows me in. Still staring at the script. 'Sorry,' he mutters, 'I've got 3 hours to learn this. Audition.' I leave him in peace and start my book.

Concorde takes off and goes supersonic after about 15 minutes. The speedometer shows an impressive Mach 1.2. That's just over the speed of sound, faster than a bullet. According to the pilot.

We're served brunch. For me, grilled sea bass with caviar sauce and a glass of champagne.

After the meal, the actor guy gets up to go to the loo, leaving his script on his seat.

Almost immediately someone plonks themselves down, picking up the script and reading it. 'You are my only love...' I look round startled. 'Chop!'

'Don you imbecile. What on Earth? You're not shadowing me for some weird reason?'

'As if!' he laughs. 'I'm going to New York to sign a contract. Biggest yet Shylock. But what's a cheapskate like doing on Concorde?'

'I won a trip it in a raffle.'

'Oh yeh? And I'm the Pope.'

I hasten to change the subject. 'Look, really why are you here?'

'Simples. George was retired, States given to me. Was on your flight to New York last week to see a Big Cheese. Diverted to Chicago. Was going to hitch back on the flight you took but rang the geezer's office to apologise and guess what?

'Don't tell me... he was delayed in Chicago too?'

'Bravo, bravo Uri... Anyway, we had dinner, did the deal and I'm spending today in JFK going through the contract with one of his henchmen. Bit of luck I'll fly back tonight with a signature.'

At which point, a hand appears and grabs the script. 'This is my seat!'

'Sorry, mate. Just wanted to catch up with Young Sterny here. Have a good trip Sternberg and enjoy your meeting with Brad!' How the fuck?

'Brad mentioned you, moron,' says God.

Brad has arranged for me to stay at a hotel owned by one of his mates. I enter the European style lobby of Gramercy Park Hotel, holding my suit carrier. I fill in my registration form with a silver Concorde pen.

A girl in a red sweater asks, 'How was your Concorde trip?'

'Amazing. Left London 10.30, arrived 09:30 at Kennedy.'

'Ain't natural,' she says in her heavy Bronx. She hands me a room key from a cubbyhole behind her. 'Have a good day.'

I sail through gilded lift doors managed by a doorman in gold braid.

As I wait for the lift, the girl at the desk waves a memo, calls to me. 'Mr Stern, message for you. Mr Randolph's so looking forward to meeting you.' She gazes at me. '*The* Brad Randolph?' Her cute green eyes dilate. 'You work for Randolph Studios?'

'Not exactly.'

'But you're meeting Brad, right?'

'Yeah...'

'Could I be an extra?'

'I'll see what I can do.'

No cable TV, fax or computer point in my room. Howling air-conditioner housed below my window. Disable the monster and stare out over the Manhattan skyline. An hour to spare. I need some fresh air.

Take the lift to the lobby and approach the smiling doorman. 'What can I do for you, Mr Stern.'

Ask if he can let me into Gramercy Park. He accompanies me across the road to the park gate. 'What time shall I let you out?' He unlocks the black, wrought iron gate with an enormous metal key.

'Give me twenty minutes, please.'

'Sure, Sir.' He locks the gate.

Pace the park's perimeter, admire rose beds, bird-house, a statue to Edwin Booth, recumbent nymphs.

After a while, I return to the black gate. No doorman. Thirty minutes later, I realize that I'm locked in Gramercy Park. If I can't get out, I'll miss my second Randolph meeting! I'm worried sick.

Two burly cops stroll past the gates. Shall I ask for help?

'This guy was trespassing!' 'Officer, I had a meeting with Brad Randolph.' Tell that one to the Judge!

They pass.

'Excuse, me.' I shout at a jogger running on the spot.

'Shh! I'm busy timing myself.'

Then Salvation. The perspiring doorman beetles over, breathing coarsely. 'I'm so sorry, Sir. Got called away, old fella checkin' out.'

Bolt back to the Hotel, shaking in the lift, run down the corridor, arrive panting at my room.

Jesus, it's almost twelve! I wrench off my clothes, run an electric razor over my cheeks and chin, quick shower, dry. I unzip my suit carrier, throw on a business suit, shirt, tie. I grab my wallet, briefcase, hurtle down to Reception, into a waiting taxi.

'713 Madison!' I bark.

The turbaned Sikh driver skids off, then looks at me in his driving mirror. 'That is Randolph Corporation?'

'Yep.'

'You visit Mr Randolph?'

'Mmm.'

'He is richer than Mr Trump.' We zigzag between speeding buses, messenger motorbikes and pedestrians.

'Eng-lish, yes? What is the weather like, England?'

Oh, for fuck's sake! Give me a silent taxi driver. He rambles on about the weather, cricket, economy, football, Bollywood.

'Here we are, mister. Your Randolph Corporation.'

'Does Randolph occupy the whole skyscraper?' I crane my head heavenwards.

'Certainly.'

I shove a ten-dollar bill through his grill. 'Keep the change.'

'You most kind.' He zooms off.

The vast atrium produces a cacophony of harsh sounds. I pass exotic palms, a café, shops, giant fountain. 'Please go to 21st,' says the Receptionist by the central lift shafts.

The doors open onto a fabulous view of Central Park, an abstract expressionist painting, an elderly woman behind a small desk. 'Welcome to New York. I'm Lucy, Mr Randolph's assistant. We spoke last week. Mr Randolph wondered whether you'd care to accompany him on a trip to Boston?'

Do I have a choice? 'That would be... wonderful.'

She makes a call. 'Mr Randolph, Mr Stern is here... yes, I'll let him know.'

'Mr Randolph will be along shortly.'

A lanky, clean-shaven cowboy swaggers towards me. 'Ricky?' Southern accent, 'sure glad you could make it. Thought we'd take a trip to Boston, get to know one another. How do you feel about that?'

'Fine, fine.'

There's a colleague directly behind him. It's Jake. 'Jake, why are we goin' to goddamn Boston?' Jake swings round, 'You bought a company there last week, remember?'

Brad puts a loving arm around him. 'That'll be that e-payments outfit, right?'

'Correct.' Jake, places his hand on Brad's lower back. 'You wanted to look it over.'

'Sure did. Now let's get goin'.'

The three of us board the lift, descend to street level. Brad strides in cowboy boots. The doorman opens the door for us.

'Teterboro Airport!' shouts Jake to the driver.

I glance at the drinks cabinet, crystal glasses, telephone, TV. A fruit bowl rests on a drinks table. Brad sprawls on one side of the seat, I sit tensely in the corner.

'You looked phased, boy. Relax, I won't bite you. By coincidence I met a friend of yours,' I feign ignorance, 'Don Smith. Said you were clever but naïve.'

'Very kind of him!' I reply almost playfully. Careful now!

'Yeh. Told me about this internet thing. Thought about bringing him on board with us, but Jake reminded me... you'd know all about that too. Right, son?'

'Absolutely Mr Randolph. Don and I worked together.'

Phew. That was a close shave. Better change the subject... Uncross my arms, loosen my jaw, roll my shoulders. Look him straight in the eyes. 'Mr Randolph, I wonder if...'

'Call me Brad, Sterny.'

'I always wondered what drives a man like you?' I ask.

'Winning drives me! Daddy was in tobacco. Soon as he died, I sold the business. Couldn't be in a trade that kills folk. In the last ten years, I've been on a worldwide media-spending spree. Now, Jake may have told you, we're looking at Telecoms. Jake says you can aid and inspire us.'

Lincoln Tunnel. A clatter, tyre squeals.

'Did he tell you 'bout my business?'

'Sure, expensive phone calls. But son, we need your mind. I hear you're real smart.'

'For I have given him a vision!' says God.

'My mind goes with me. I go with the business.'

He slaps his thigh. 'Ha! So tell me, how'd you get us into Telecoms into the States, son?'

'You mean straightforward telephone calls?'

'What other sort of calls are there?' he asks, seemingly intrigued.

Well, we do Premium Calls, expensive calls that..' he looks bored already.

I change tack. 'Straight telephone calls – at a discount, you mean?'

'Now you're talking!' His face lights up.

'As it happens, I was thinking about launching something like that in the UK. National Sentinel and Randolph Studios viewers would dial a four-digit code before each call to get a discount.' I pontificate.

He takes me through the minutiae of my idea and bombards me with questions.

'Each caller gets a discount off the standard Telecom rate,' I explain.

'Like how much?'

'20%.'

Not enough. I want 50%!'

We speed through New Jersey streets, and into an industrial estate. Ahead of us, a steel perimeter fence and a sign, 'Teterboro Airport.'

'One last question,' says Brad, 'How do you go about setting this up in the States?'

'I'd need to research this further.' I'm honest enough to admit that.

'You'd better get on with it.' He thumps me on the back.

We clamber aboard the Gulfstream. Pilot, a handsome Southern redneck says, 'Welcome aboard, Gentlemen.'

'Howdy, Steve.' Brad, shakes his hand, clasps his arm, 'How's the weather doin'?'

'No probs, Mr Randolph, we'll be airborne in under ten minutes.'

A stewardess in a mauve tunic takes our coats. Jake lumbers over and collapses into a sofa. His shirt needs pressing, his brown shoes are scuffed. Brad crashes in the large fawn chair next to mine.

'Ricky, here,' he leans over and prods my shoulder with his fist, 'wants to put ATT outta business. So boy, what'll we have to do for you to join our empire?'

The jet shoots into the air. Jake folds his paper and throws it on the table. 'He's already got a company. Irony, a VC hold 30%. But why does he need us?'

Brad rubs his chin with a massive ringed hand. Ignores the question. 'How much they take to go?'

'We'll make £150k profit this year,' I reply. 'Based on ten times pre-tax profits. That'll value my company Ring-Inn at £1.5m.'

'What did they invest?' asks Brad.

'£300k, half-equity, half-debt.'

'Any loan outstanding?'

'Nope.'

'When was the investment made?'

'Three years ago.'

'Hmm, not bad. They'll walk away with half a million pounds for an investment of £150k.'

What about my stake? Homeless...

'Guess you're reckonin' on us payin' you £1m for your share?' Well, err, yes. 'We need you to stay and sweat the business. After you've made us both some dough, we promise to make you rich.'

'I need to cash a few of my shares now.' Otherwise, I'll have Sonny and his henchmen down my throat, re-possessing my home.

'What exactly d'you have in mind?'

'You buy 35% of my shares now. Keep me in at 35%.'

'Let me think about that, Boy. How much additional business could you do if all our UK titles and Randolph Studios gave you full cooperation?'

'Five-fold increase.'

'Very impressive,' says Brad. Jake shows him the total displayed on his calculator. 'Tell you what,' continues Brad, 'We'll keep you in at 25%, pay you for your 45% over 2 years.'

'That's almost £700k in total,' says Jake.

'Sounds fine,' I reply. *Stuff your mortgage, Sonny!*

'Fasten your seatbelts,' orders the pilot Steve through the intercom. The plane taxis to a halt. The stewardess returns our coats. Steve bids us farewell. 'See you at 3 p.m. gentlemen.'

As my feet hit the tarmac, I whisper to Jake, 'What happened then?'

He takes my arm, says softly, 'You sold your company to Randolph Corporation. We'll send the auditors in next week.'

A double-stretched limo awaits us. We pile in and sprawl around its darkened interior. A black plastic grill separates us from a uniformed chauffeur. He slides open the grille, 'Where to, gentlemen?'

Jake wrestles with his organizer, peers at the screen, 'Massachusetts, near Porter.'

Brad examines closing prices in the *Wall Street Journal*. 'What do I do next?' I ask him.

He glances over the paper and mumbles, 'You'd best meet Ginger Fox...'

Jake explains, 'He's CEO of our UK operations. Based in London. I'll fix it.'

I sit in silence while Randolph boasts of his latest acquisition, and Jake of his weight loss diet. Commander Stern glides through Boston boulevards, honoured guest of Brad Megabucks. Skyscrapers sail by long tinted limo window.

'What number?' shouts the driver.

They shrug. 'There it is!' Jake points at a humble concrete block across the street.

'Can't make a turn,' sighs the driver. 'Road's too narrow.'

'Don't worry,' says Brad, 'We'll get out here, walk back, do our hearts a world of good.'

Cars hoot at our limo, blocking the road. Brad strides out across the street. I wait for a pause in the traffic. The guy in the car behind hoots, 'Say, isn't that Brad Randolph?'

And a still, small voice replies, 'With him is Commander Stern.'

20

I cross Berkeley Square, walk to the Randolph Corporation building. Office drones slurp coffee, lovers cuddle, flowers bloom.

At Security, 'Yes Sir, we're expecting you, 7th floor.' I stick their VIP badge onto my tie, take the lift. A motherly woman with bouffant silver hair, a tweed suit and blue-rimmed specs guards Ginger Fox.

'Hi, I'm Veronica. Guess we'll be seeing a lot of you, from now on. Coffee?' She gestures to the office behind her. 'Ginge's finishing a meeting. Take a pew.'

I sit under a flattering portrait of cowboy Brad Randolph and glance through today's National Sentinel. Veronica disappears into a kitchenette. I have an eagle-eyed view of other floors – a busy, open-plan editorial unit, brawny workmen in overalls fix a lift.

Veronica returns with a Randolph Corporation mug for me. She fields calls, types on screen. I replace the newspaper on the coffee table, glance at Saratoga Times, peer across at Veronica's possessions: Large black diary, white printed internal directory.

Ginger's frosted glass door swings open. A procession of morose executives file out. 'We'll never make budget,' a depressed voice says.

'Crazy!' says another.

A voice bellows, 'Send in the impostor!'

'Better go in,' Veronica whispers.

Ginger Fox stands in front of his desk, arms akimbo. 'Let's take a peek at you then!'

I shuffle in. A white melamine table is piled high with used coffee cups, half-eaten biscuits, sugar wrappers.

'Let me shake your hand.' A hyena strides towards me, paw outstretched from a blue shirtsleeve. I transfer my coffee mug to my left hand, grasp his right.

He clenches my hand in both paws. 'You need congratulatin', me old China.'

'Thank you,' I reply.

'That all you've to say for yourself?' He slams the door shut; it rattles. 'I've checked you out. You're a nuffin. Yet, somehow, you've hoodwinked Brad into thinkin' you're a fuckin' genius. You can't fool me. And you've conned the Boss into payin' you more than I'll earn in a lifetime, slogging me guts out, year after year.'

He clutches his wavy red mane, paces head down, past green sofa, dark oak bookcase, Kentia palm.

'Err, sorry,' I mumble.

'Now he's sorry. One minute he's happy, next fuckin' sorry. Sit, pillock!' He gestures to the chair near gingernut cookies.

He collapses on his seat, unbuttons his shirt, stretches out his check-clad legs, pivots, stares at the wall-mounted National Sentinel front pages, celebrity photos, Newspaper of the Year Award.

'Keep schtum!' God warns me.

'Pass me a bikky,' he orders and chews thoughtfully. I could be at the Electricity Commission with Ken Smith. Has anything changed?

He rises, slumps in the chair next to mine, snarls, 'Because we've a common cause, I'll do what's good for the business. I'd always do that. We'll carry your premium numbers. But 'part from that, my job's to discourage you, block your initiatives, ensure you don't make a penny more than your miserable salary. This'll be our little secret. Have you met Tony, yet?'

'Tony?'

'You're in for a treat.' He grabs his phone handset. 'Tony, old bean. Pop in here a mo', there's someone special I want you to meet.' Receiver crashes down on its cradle. 'Tony's in business development. He's your new Managing Director.'

'I've got a Managing Director.' I feel giddy.

He kicks my shins. 'Demote or fire them. Your choice, of course,' he smirks, all heart.

A breathless 30-something pops his tousled head around the door. 'You wanted me, Ginge?'

'Yeah, yeah.'

Tony, an anorexic owl walks towards us, eyes me. Creased white shirt, crumpled gold tie. 'Tony Hastings, meet Ricky Stern. We've taken over his company. What's it called Ricko? Oh, I recall, Ring-Inn. Stupid name.'

'Ring what?' asks Tony.

'Premium Rate lines.'

'Oh, I get it,' replies Tony. I wonder if he's got a clue...

Ginger sits upright, 'Tone's one of our fast-track MBAs, ain't you, Tone.'

I have a religious objection to MBAs. 'Where did you study?' I ask.

'INSEAD, Paris.' Should have guessed.

Ginger thumps Tony's shoulder, 'I'm placing you in the battlefield, Tone. You're now Managing Director of Ring-Inn... it's not a serious name, is it Ricko. We'll re-name it Randolph Phone Communications.'

He points at Tony. 'From now on you're based at... What did I call the bugger?'

'RPC,' says Tony.

'Ah, yes. In Pinner,' continues Ginger.

'Camden,' I interject.

Ginger leans against his desk, wags index finger 'Tone, I want you to downsize, cost-cut, rationalise, re-locate, sweat assets and maximise... read my lips... profits. All our titles should carry *his* numbers. I want regular reports. If *he* goes to the toilet, I wanna know.'

'Yes, Ginge,' Tony faces me. 'Ricky, can I come across this afternoon?'

'Sure, look forward to it. Here's my card.'

Ginger jumps up, 'I'll come too. Ought to see the far-thest reaches of our Empire. New York, L.A, Sydney... now grotty Camden. What's the weather like?' asks Gin-ger.

Tony mutters, 'Don't have a card with me, but switchboard can always find me. Cheers!' He waves feebly, exits.

'Nice chap, don't you think?' Ginger taps my elbow. 'Ambitious, know-what-I-mean?'

All too well.

'Ginge, I was hoping we could work with Randolph Studios.'

He skips across the room. 'Were you, Sunshine? Only the UK's largest fuckin' satellite channel. Guess you'd make millions from that?'

'And for the company.'

He stops by the biscuits, 'Nah!' Devours one. 'Do too little, business suffers. Too much, you get rich. Can't have that. We're talking life sentence, no escape. You'd better see Human Resources and Finance about our company car policy. Oh, and one last thing...'

'What's that?' I gasp.

'The Boss calls you,' he prods my chest, 'you call me. Geddit?' As I leave, he adds, 'Welcome to Randolph Corporation, boyo!'

Veronica smiles, 'Ginge's a lovely man, isn't he?'

'Absolutely charming.'

I'm desolate and demoralised. *Life sentence, discourage, block your initiatives.* I stroll back through Regent's Park and stand by the fountains in the Rose Garden. I'm trapped again. My alternatives: Struggle with Ginger or work for Susie's dad selling carpets. No choice.

Into bloody battle! I run to the Inner Circle, hail a passing taxi, pound upstairs to my office. Meg greets me in a black mini-dress, matching shoes, newly-cropped, black hair. Hard to believe, she'll soon be a pensioner.

'We're having a Grand Visitation,' I announce to her and Accounts.

'A *séance?'* she laughs.

'No, Ginger Fox, CEO of Randolph UK, visiting us at 6 p.m. Can you stay on a bit later? Inform management.'

She reluctantly agrees.

'Oh and please instruct Des to wear his bloody uniform.'

She clutches a white A4 to her bosom, gives it to me. 'It's from Gavin, for you.'

I tear it open and read:

<u>PARKING FINES</u>

May 3rd	£1000
May 5th	£2000
May 6th(two breaches)	£4000 and £8000
May 7th	£16000
Total	£31000
VAT	£5425
TOTAL including VAT	£36425

'He's gotta be joking!' I shout.

She replies glumly, 'When you were in the States, folk took liberties. Gavin was on the case with his camera.'

Gavin *and* Ginger are on my back. What a treat!

'Good luck!' She says as I crash through the Fire Exit, rush downstairs, leap the last few steps, press Gavin's bell hard.

'What's all the fuss? I'm having a *siesta*,' barks the intercom.

'You... you... shit.' I scream.

'My, my! What passion! I'll put the kettle on.'

I dash into his deserted workroom. Snaps of the courtyard are pinned to the diagonal beam over his desk.

'Gavin?' I call.

'Won't be a mo', just puttin' on me trousers for battle,' he calls gaily from the bedroom, 'Chamomile tea will calm you down.'

On his desk, a pile of scripts, each rubber-stamped across with Gleam Toothpaste. I run my index finger along with the titles of books in an oak bookcase. Jeffrey Archer, *Urban Renewal, The Brotherhood, National Geographics*.

'Feel free to borrow,' Gavin appears in Moroccan slippers with two mugs. 'Now what's the problem?' He sets the tea down on his desk and sits in his functional metal chair facing me. The breeze from the canal window cools my neck.

'This!' I flick the Parking Fines document across the table. He doesn't look down.

'I'll give you 30 days to pay. How's that for generosity?'

'You can't fine us arbitrary amounts; I've checked with my lawyer. What would there be to stop you charging £100,000?'

He giggles. 'By my calculations, two more transgressions. £128,000, to be precise.'

'It's madness! I'm not putting it through our books. I'm prepared to settle for a reasonable sum of £250.'

He sips his chamomile tea, calmness itself. 'Out of the question. Pay up in full or else.'

'Else what? We're now part of Randolph Corporation. They'll tell you to go shit yourself.'

He stares at rafters, 'Or I'll switch your electricity off at 6 p.m. tonight.'

'6 p.m! But that's when... Gavin, you cunt, you've been bugging my office again.'

He turns deep crimson. 'I warn you, one more accusation like that and I'll sue.'

'There's no point in continuing this conversation. £250 is my best offer. If you shut off our electricity, I'll get an injunction, sue you for loss of earnings.' I leave my chamomile tea untouched, storm out and stride breathlessly back up to my office.

As I pass Meg, I bark, 'Strong coffee, get Gary up here immediately.'

I poke the base of the bamboo plant, supplied by Office Greenery. No recorder. I crawl under my desk, yank off my phone cover. No obvious tap.

Gary strides in, 'Something up?' He slouches on the sofa, hands behind his head.

'We've got the head honcho of Randolph Corporation coming over at 6 p.m. and, by a remarkable coincidence, bloody Gavin's threatening to cut off our electricity if we don't pay his extortionate parking fines.'

Gary smiles. 'Let him try, we've got UPS.'

'Isn't that a parcel service?'

'Uninterruptible Power Supply. It trips in if there's a power outage on the local supply.'

'Surely, that's only for the machine-room.'

'Correct, but we have a standby generator for lights and PCs.'

'Wow!' Commander Stern into action. 'Can you test backup systems?'

'Sure. I'll let you know.'

'Also, the Telecom box in the forecourt. Make sure there's no recording device hooked to it.'

'You don't think you're being bugged, do you?' asks Gary, naïve, wide-eyed.

'You can't be too careful these days.'

He commiserates with my anxiety. 'Well, I'll get on with things straight away, OK?' He strides out.

A few minutes later, he calls to tell me the standby generator's working and there's no tap on our junction box.

Throughout the afternoon, Meg and freelancers scrub desks and PCs, ensure full toilet rolls, arrange fresh flowers and spray the building with lavender. Gary rushes to Boots to buy a disposable razor to shave his unruly beard. Tessa disappears into the loo to further beautify herself. Terry has a nap on the reception sofa. 'Put your bloody alarm on for 5:30 p.m. Terry!'

Des arrives late afternoon in a pressed uniform, with a white carnation in his lapel, shiny silver buttons, polished black boots, hair trimmed and combed.

He stands erect outside the entrance as we assemble for the Grand Visitation. At precisely 6 p.m. a black Mercedes drives into the forecourt, parks directly in front of the steps. A chauffeur with peaked cap springs out, opens the rear door. Ginger emerges into the sunshine. Tony lets himself out from another door.

As Ginger ascends the steps, we form a line to greet him like his servants. Halfway up, he stops to admire the flower baskets and a fine view of the canal. 'Cor, you got quite a place here Stern.'

'Thanks. I'd like you to meet Terry, Gary, Tessa and Meg.' Ginger and Tony shake hands with the assembled team.

'Send my regards to Brad,' Terry says.

Ginger eyes him suspiciously. 'You know 'im then?'

'Sure, Brad and I went white water rafting in Nebraska last year.'

'Really? What you say your name was?'

'Err, hmm,' a disembodied voice rises from behind Ginger.

'Oh, and this is Des, our Night Guard.'

'Your Excellency,' says Des. I wince. Ginger shakes his hand warmly.

I lead the parade through the offices. First stop, computer room.

'Blimey, you make all that dosh, with this little baby. I'm obviously in the wrong job.' Exclaims Ginger. For once he sounds sincere.

Nervous titters all around.

'Let's see your office, Ricko.'

The procession marches upstairs. Ginger enters, eyes agog. 'It's far bigger than mine! You can't even see the far end of it.' He runs his hands along oak beams. 'It's the genuine McCoy. No cement and concrete for our Sterny.' He strolls around, straightens my sepia etchings of Old Hampstead. He stands in the centre of my office, and gushes, 'A regular Palace. I'm impressed.'

'Shall we retire to the Boardroom?' I suggest. He takes a deep breath, exhales. 'Sure, why not?'

Ginger, Tony and I sit at one end of the long Board table, the others distribute themselves around. Meg pours champagne.

'A toast... to Randolph Corporation.' We all stand, raise and clink glasses. Meg waves goodbye, mouths 'Good luck,' to me, slips out.

'I wish to say,' announces Ginger, 'that we at Randolph, are delighted to be working with RPC.'

'RPC?' asks Terry.

'Randolph Phone Corporation, that will replace... what in hell's name was it?' He looks my way.

'Ring-Inn,' I say.

'Yeah. We respect the culture your Ricky has developed and it's our intention to support your activities with the minimum intervention. Tony here,' Tony sits erect, grins, 'is your new Managing Director.'

'But I'm Managing Director!' interjects Gary.

'Yeah, whatever...' Ginger's mask slips.

The lights flicker. Has Gavin cut the power?

A face peers through the glass of the Boardroom door. There's a knock and Gavin creeps in.

'Excuse me, everyone.'

'Who are *you*?' scowls Ginger.

'I'm Gavin Penhaligon, the landlord here.'

'I know your face! You're the guy in the toothpaste commercial. What's it called?' asks Ginger.

'Gleam,' replies a bashful Gavin.

'What d'yer know?' He prods me, then Tony. 'His smile's so bright, he knocks birds off their bikes! So, what do you want then?'

'It's the Limo, parked against regulations.'

Ginger scowls. 'What bloody regulations?'

'Your lease. I must bring your attention to the fact that your tenant,' he nods my way, 'refuses to pay his fines?'

I'll drag Gavin to the top of the building, tie a lump of concrete to his feet, dump him in the canal.

'Won't pay your fines, Sunshine?' He kicks me under the table.

'We lease three car parking spaces. Gavin's trying to fine us £36,000. While I was visiting Brad in the States, staff took liberties.'

'£36,425 to be exact.' A smug Gavin guards the door. Ginger looks around the dismayed faces. Pin-drop silence.

'That's over £7,000 a pop!'

'Inclusive of VAT.'

Ginger stomps over to Gavin. 'It includes VAT! You off your fuckin' trolley? Think we were born yesterday?' He turns to me. 'What do the lawyers say, Ricko?'

'He doesn't have a leg. Maybe £250 total is appropriate.' At least there's an upside to working with Randolph. 'He tried to blackmail us by turning off our electricity, but we've standby generators. They're running now.'

'Well, well, well!' snorts Ginger.

A bright-pink Gavin says, 'If we don't settle amicably, I shall refuse to renew the lease.'

'When's that up?'

'December 26th,' replies Gavin.

'That'll make a great goodwill Christmas present,' says Ginger.

'What will?' asks a perplexed Gavin.

'Us moving out.'

'Moving out?' Gavin's on the run.

Ginger pauses for maximum impact. 'Yeah, Randolph's openin' a new site in Northampton. We need additional tenants. We could move this whole lot.' He waves at Management.

Northampton! The staff look glum.

'I'm sure we can sort something reasonable out,' says a shocked Gavin.

'Yeah? For a start, we'll forget the fake fines and you'll turn the electrics back on. Now, scarper!'

Gavin exits, embarrassed.

'Tone, make a note.' Tony scrambles for his brief-case, pulls out a loose-leaf notepad, 'Find out who owns the building. Buy it. We'll cut that bastard out of the equation.'

'So, we're not moving to Northampton?' I ask.

'Did I say Northampton? Nah, it would be too grand a set-up for your motley crew.'

21

Tony sits at the head of the table, with me beside him. Gary arrives immaculately groomed. Tessa wears a black power suit. Terry's dapper, as always.

Our Finance Director Basil rushes in late.

An expectant management stare at me, as I open the meeting. 'Welcome to our first Executive meeting as part of Randolph Corporation. You've met Tony, our Chief Executive Officer.' He raises one hand. 'I'll be handing day-to-day business to him. He'll Chair today.'

Gary scowls. Tessa smiles at me. Terry blows his nose on a white linen handkerchief.

Tony's elbows rest on the table. 'Thanks, Rick. I'd like to congratulate you *all* on your outstanding performance. I've asked Basil to reformat our management reports on Group lines. When will they be ready, Baz?'

'Next week, hopefully,' Baz mumbles, jotting.

'Terrific. Can you give us an overview?'

Baz shuffles reports, selects one. 'Revenue's £90k, profit £12k.'

'Thanks,' continues Tony. 'Tessa?'

She flutters her eyelashes. 'After our difficulties with the Universe promotion... revenue fell.'

'Difficulties?' interrupts Tony.

'Our fuckin' lines were sabotaged!' Terry bangs the table.

'No back-up?' says Tony.

Gary says, 'We didn't have time...' Minus 5 points. Tony makes a note.

'Can you write a full account of what happened? List what measures should be taken in the future?'

The workplace used to be fun. Now we're a bunch of monkeys. I fantasise about a new life on a Greek island with Tessa as my Girl Friday.

'Anyway,' continues Tessa, 'Universe cut our Astrology lines and moved them to Phoneworks. They're also replacing Racing.'

Tony jots, tilts his chair back, 'Universe is owned by Sargant Communications. Sargant loathes us. We can expect to lose all their business, but we'll more than replace it with National Sentinel services.'

'Terry, the overheads on Racing... do we have to cover every race? How 'bout outsourcing.'

An apoplectic Terry pinches his Adam's apple, rubs his purple face. 'Not cover every race? You fuckin' jokin'? Didn't they teach you anything at that fancy French place? Incy-somethin'?'

'INSEAD? I heard Sports Press Services had approached us.'

'They're fuckin' amateurs.'

Tony scowls. 'Can I see their proposal, please?'

'Jezuz!'

Tensions rise. Terry drums his fingers, doodles a hangman. 'Basil, which among this lot has a company car?'

Basil stops jotting, gives Tony his full attention. 'Terry, Gary, Tessa. Ricky gets a cash equivalent. The sales staff... I'll make you a list.'

Tony relaxes. He's established control. 'Ta. Wanna make sure we all conform to Group Car Policy.'

Group fucking car policy.

Tess flutters her eyelashes at bachelor Tony. I'm jealous. 'Tony? Can you approach Randolph Studios? We could make squillions together.'

'I asked Ginger Fox to call. He's working on it, says it's political.'

'What's fuckin' political about it?' asks Terry.

'They want to run it themselves.'

My heart sinks. That way, I make nothing. Never trusted that bastard Fox or his cronies.

After the meeting, Terry stomps behind me into my office. 'You're in league with the Devil. Whatever fuckin' possessed you?' He flings his blazer over the back of my leather couch, slumps on it, arms raised sideways.

'I had to pay off my mortgage. You've a short memory.'

He shakes his head. 'I'm not hanging around any longer.'

'What? You can't leave. Benny went last month when Universe switched contracts to Phoneworks. Can't you wait to see how things pan out?'

'I'm not working with a masochistic, humourless spider,' shouts Terry.

'Oh, thanks very much.'

He cackles. 'That stuffed shirt, Incyweeny. I'm even considering emigrating to Oz.'

'The Outback? Why?'

'Bin offered a job frontin' a Channel Nine TV show. Bin chasin' me for months. Didn't want to let you down, but now...' He shakes his head. 'Need to review my options. Sorry, Ricky.'

I won't even try to stop him.

'I'll miss you terribly.' I confess.

We hug by my desk. I shut my bleary eyes.

'Uh-hum,' coughs a voice.

I dab my face with a tissue. 'Oh, Tony. Come in. Bad news, Terry's leaving.' Tony beams.

'Well, I'll be off. I'll work out me three months' notice, of course,' Terry says.

'Good of you,' I say as he slinks off.

'What can I do for you, Tony?' I gesture at the couch. He takes Terry's place.

'How much did *he* earn?'

'Tel? 80 grand or thereabouts.'

He rubs his hands gleefully. 'Great. That's a result, well done!'

I pace over to the Fire Exit, 'I didn't fire him!'

'Whatever. The Group wants me to squeeze overheads by 20%.'

'Will that be all, Tony?'

'That hobo on reception.'

'Des? You want to lay him off also?'

'Group policy. We subcontract to Security Contracts.'

Even spiders have more humour. 'Couldn't Des transfer to them?'

'Strangely enough, they don't hire ex-cons.'

Sarcastic lemming.

'Darling, you sleeping?' I whisper.

'Not again… What time is it?' Fumble, fumble, '3 o'clock, you're not casting another spell, are you?'

I prop myself up on an elbow. 'Don't know why you're complaining. It worked, didn't it?'

'You certainly sold your business to old Megabucks. I confess it's remarkable. But spells? The whole idea's weird.' She pulls the duvet over her face, snuggles under it.

'I'd appreciate your advice.'

'Not now. Get some sleep.'

'Can't.'

'Oh, what is it?' She sits up.

I grab my specs from my bedside table. The London skyline glitters. She lies on my chest, cuddles me.

'You know I made a small fortune from the first tranche of Randolph Corporation money. Well, after paying Mr Taxman, Urban Mortgages and our outstanding debts, we've about £300k. If I stay on at Randolph, I've got the chance to make a couple of million more.

But they are driving me stark raving bonkers. Ginge is a schizo-psychopath. Tone's as much fun as fried onion.'

'So leave. We'll make do.' She sighs, rubs my chest through my jimjams.

'Losers unto the Tenth Generation...'

'I'm going to beat the bastards at their own bloody game!'

'Suit yourself, lovey. Now sleep.' She rolls back to her side of the bed, asleep in minutes.

My status at Randolph Corporation HQ equips me with a corporate power-badge: 'Access All Areas.' I flash my Technicolour mug shot to the doorman, who says, 'Go right ahead, Mr Stern.' I run the badge's magnetic stripe through a reader. Twin doors click open.

The Executive floor at Berkeley Square is a hive of hushed inactivity.

I pop my head into the first office, 'Excuse me, I'm looking for a Fiona Wallace.'

Officious dragon eyes me with distrust. 'Third office to the right,' she spits. Corporate body language for, 'Fiona's a conniving bitch.'

Fiona might be a key ally in my attempt to extract further dough from Randolph Corporation, but she's dangerous – *Handle With Care*. She's an elegant beauty with a long neck, pearl necklace, musk scent. She stands and chats to her seccie.

She turns as I enter. 'Ricky, darling.' Kiss on both cheeks, 'Congratulations! Not many men get the better of our Brad.' Is she a Sloane Ranger, sleeping with the cowboy, Ginger or both? 'Come through.'

Her boudoir is alive with modernist art, a green chaise lounge, designer wallpaper, gilt-framed mirror, arranged roses on a dainty antique coffee table. Her mahogany desk is clear, except for a small notebook, embossed with 'FAW,' topped with a Mont Blanc pen.

'What a great pad. I could live here,' I say.

'Is that a proposition?' She bats green eyes set in pale flawless skin. She lifts her long legs onto her desk for me to admire. Caution!

I leap across the table, knock the table lamp flying, peel off her black dress and tights, screw her under a Kokoshka nude.

'Brad told me you're gonna transform Randolph Corporation into a Telco. I asked Ginge about you. He suggested I get to know you better. Help to oil wheels in the Corporation, seeing as I'm Director of Group Strategy.'

It's a steel trap. I search her eyes for signs of shiftiness, but she looks back at me with a steady gaze.

'I'm trying my best,' I say, 'but it's not easy.'

'Tell me about it,' she purrs.

If Fiona's sleeping with Brad, she won't have much time for Ginge. 'It's Ginger,' I confess nervously.

'That loser,' she says.

Wow.

'If only Ginge would help me with Randolph Studios.'

'Why not go directly to the horse?'

'Ginger's warned me not to approach Brad directly.'

'What if you just happened to be having a drink at the Stafford tonight, around 7 p.m. waiting for a friend say...'

'I couldn't do that, could I?'

She winks. 'Leave it to me.'

I creep into the Stafford bar at 6.55 p.m. excited, duplicitous, heart palpitating. Order a Scotch. I rarely drink. Reckless decision.

'Make that two,' a familiar voice, a claw drilled into my back.

Eeek!

'Didn't know you were in town, Brad.'

'Flying visit, dinner at Downing. *He* wants Sentinel to change its stance on Europe.'

A couple of regulars point at Brad's Stetson and tut-tut. Gold cufflinks, blue denim shirt.

'And would you?' I ask.

'Let's say we'd trade Europe, for a little understanding on the satellite front.'

The barman presents two whiskeys. Brad takes a hit. I sip slowly, plan to ingratiate myself, not get *schiker*.

'What else?' I ask.

'Yesterday was in Russia. You've seen nuffin' like it. Americans everywhere. MacDonald's, ATT, you name it. But I wanna know how your idea's getting on. You're putting Telecom out of business. Right?'

'It's hopeless. I can't get a meeting with Randolph Studios.'

'I'll sort that out. Call tomorrow.' He downs his whiskey. 'Can't keep your PM waiting. Put this on my tab, Victor,' he commands barman. 'See ya tomorrow, kiddo. And by the way,' he grabs my arm, 'I wanna see a plan for the States. That'll be between us, son. Don't tell Ginge!'

Arghh..

Next morning...

For damage limitation, I best tell Ginger, before Brad gets to him. I call Veronica and learn our Ginge's breakfasting with Brad. Yikes, I'm toast!

Twenty minutes later Ginger calls me. 'You menace! You're fuckin' trouble! Skivin' off behind my back and sucking up to Brad,' screams Ginger. I hold the receiver away from my ear.

'Ginge, it was a coincidence.'

'Coincidence! Bollocks! What do you do? Hang around St. James's? You musta bin waitin' a long time. He hasn't been to London for weeks. Get a life!'

'I was waiting for a friend and Brad walks in.'

'Crap! Hang on, hang on. You was tipped off, sunshine, yes?'

'Not at all.'

'Who by? Don't tell me. That cow Fiona Wallace.'

'Why would she do that?'

'You two were made for each other.'

'So now?'

'We've ALL got a cosy fuckin' 3 p.m. meeting. And that includes you, sunshine!'

Oi Vey.

If Ginger has his way, my time at Randolph will be short-lived. I take the lift up to the 7th Floor.

'Go straight in,' says Veronica.

Brad and Ginger huddle around a melamine table. Brad demolishes a banana. Ginger, a ginger biscuit.

'Here's the maestro,' says Ginger, 'grab a seat. Vee, clear the wreckage, please.'

Veronica whooshes in with a tray, spirits away sandwich packets, half-drunk coffee mugs, a fruit bowl.

'Howdy, partner,' says Brad, studying a spreadsheet. He turns it over and lays it on the table.

'Ginge, what do Randolph Studios say about Rick's idea?'

'They're unimpressed, Boss. Want to do something themselves, not RPC.'

'RPC?' asks Brad.

'Yeah, we thought Ring-Inn naff. Renamed it Randolph Phone Communications.'

'I thought Ring-Inn was fine,' says Brad.

'So did I,' I chime in. Ginger throws me a dagger's look.

Brad strolls to the open door, 'Vee, get me Larry Higgins at Randolph Studios, PDQ.'

The phone rings on Ginger's desk. Brad picks it up. 'Larry, it's Brad. How yer doin'?.. I'm fine too. 'Listen, Larry, we've acquired a phone company… R…'

'RPC,' mouths Ginger.

'RPC. Ricky Stern's running it. Knows all there is to know and some… Yeah, Ginger told me. Unless I'm missin' sumfin', none of your development guys have ever run a business. As I said, it's your call. Maybe you should meet Ricky, see how you get on.' He replaces the receiver.

Randolph Studios is based in Wembley industrial waste-land, near the North Circular. The cab disgorges me at the central reception block. I show my pass. 'It doesn't work here, Sir. Have to ask you to sign in,' says the pert receptionist. 'Take a seat, Sir.'

If I pull off a deal with Randolph Studios, I'll be made.

I goggle at a bank of screens: News, *Friends,* Man United highlights, Elton John video. A young lass greets me. 'Hi, I'm Shane, Uncle Larry's niece and assistant.'

She looks twelve. 'Shouldn't you be at school?'

'It's half-term. Uncle asked me to help out while his PA's on a training course.'

She leads me through a maze of corridors into a room with green backlighting, walls, even a green door handle. A view of a small pond with bamboo shoots and a fountain is lit by green floodlight. Soothing New Age melodies. A running machine stands in a corner.

The most eccentric man in British TV sits on a green sofa watching cartoons, munching a carrot.

'Hello, lad,' strong Geordie accent, 'won't be two ticks.' He's entranced. 'New show we're pilotin'. Wanna carrot?' He points to a bowl and I take one. I sink into a green armchair to watch aliens devour Mars. Larry guf-faws, slaps thighs.

'Summat to drink?' asks Shane. 'Organic lemonade, beetroot juice or nettle tea?'

'Any normal tea?'

''Fraid not.'

Larry silences the TV with his remote, 'We've nought with caffeine, Laddie. Fancy water?'

'I'll try nettle.'

Shane skips off.

Larry addresses me. 'Well, laddie, what 've you to say for yerself then?'

I wave my hand. 'What's with the green?'

'It's God's own colour.'

Shane returns balancing a tray precariously. She places a cup and tall glass on a green plastic toadstool. Larry sips juice through a straw. 'I hear you know all about phones? Fire away.'

Commander Stern, Telephone Guru to media moguls.

'What's your wee plan?'

I start my *spiel*, 'We could develop an integrated telephone service to compete with cable companies... '

He strokes his chin. 'Can we now? Tell me now, how do we achieve such a miracle?'

'Viewers dial a code 1808.'

'Aye.' He nibbles his carrot and fires questions at me for ten minutes. 'You certainly know your stuff. How much will you want for this miracle?'

'I don't want payment. We'll make money from each call. I'll share it with you.'

'How much d'you reckon for starters?'

'Ten million.'

He shoves my arm off the armrest. 'Give over! That, on a 50/50 basis?'

'Yep.'

'Make that 60/40 in our favour, and we have got a deal.'

I hold out my hand. 'Deal.'

He leaps up, shakes my hand vigorously. This guy's about to make me very rich. Randolph Studios deal will increase turnover by £20 million. My remaining shareholding will rocket in value.

He returns to staring at the screens.

I mumble, 'Bye now'. He nods his head.

Bid farewell to Shane. Exit...

Fiona wears a demure, white silk dress. She fidgets with her silver necklace.

'Hi, stranger.' Kiss, kiss. 'Hear you sorted Randolph Studios.'

'I want to thank you, personally.'

'Come in. Something to drink?'

'Nettle tea, please.'

She squawks, 'You've been spending too much time with old Larry! He's a freakin' freak.'

I squeeze her elbow. 'I'd love a real cuppa.'

'I'll put the kettle on,' says her assistant.

Fiona beckons me into her office, shuts the door behind her. 'Come over to the couch, it's more comfortable.' She relaxes on her chaise longue, I perch six inches away from her. She uses her charm expertly, but she'll never topple Ginger. Her power will evaporate when she ceases to amuse Brad.

Her PA enters and places cups of tea on a marble coffee table. Fiona waits until she leaves, hisses. 'Did you tell Ginge?'

'About your Brad tip off?' She nods. 'He guessed it was you.' She slaps the sofa.

'Damn! We'll have to be more careful in future.'

'Careful? What are we doing?' She picks up her Mont Blanc pen, sucks it. 'How else can I help, Ricky?'

'Ah, there's one thing you could do... ' Her eyes light up. 'I'm not sure I should tell you... '

She rests her hand on my knee. 'You have to now, Ricky.'

'Then I'll have to arrange to have you bumped off!'

'Don't keep me in suspense!' she laughs.

This could be the end of me. Brad asked me to draw up a plan for the States, to keep my mission confidential. I haven't a clue where to start and limited time to deliver. I must take a chance.

'Brad asked me to investigate a certain project, in secret.'

'Then you can definitely tell me!' she laughs.

'He asked me to produce a telecoms plan for the States. Foolishly, I agreed, but I've no contacts there, and time's running out.'

She thrusts her fountain pen at me, 'I know someone. My godfather, Elias Fotherington.' Elias Fotherington? Whatta mouthful! 'He's a bit doddery, but his mind's alert. He was comms advisor to the last Administration. Acts as a consultant nowadays.'

'Where's he based?'

She whispers. 'Washington D.C.'

The door swings open, Ginger's flushed face appears. 'Oh, I'm sorry to spoil your little tryst! I dart up from the chaise longue.

'Come in, Ginger,' says Fiona calmly, 'I was just explaining the company's history to our Ricky here.'

His eyes shift from her to me. 'Sure that's true, Fi. Delighted to find you two have hit it off. Heel, Ricko.'

As I follow him, I call to Fiona, 'Our history lesson will have to wait.'

As Ginger bounds up the draughty stairwell ahead of me, I ask, 'How did you know she and I were in conference?'

He pauses on the landing and snarls. 'Walls have ears. I asked Tony, Sunshine.'

Dirty spy behind enemy lines!

I lean on the bannister, try to catch my breath, 'But I didn't tell Tone.'

'Didn't you? Perhaps he's psychic.' He strides to Veronica's desk where she sits typing. She says, 'Oh, hi Ricky. Congratulations on Randolph Studios!'

Ginger thumps my back, 'Yeah, our regular hero.' He grasps my arm. 'He won't be needing tea, will you, Rick?' He frogmarches me into his office.

Ginger slams the door, strides to his desk, slumps over PC screen to check emails, mutters, 'What you doin' next week?'

Commander Stern is due to travel First Class the States, on a secret assignment known only to himself and Lord Megabucks.

'Going to the States. Vacation. Haven't had a break for two years.' I sit at the vast conference table, help myself to a dry Chocolate Digestive.

He peers round the screen, over rimless reading specs. 'Really? Why's that? Where you off to?'

Think swiftly, Commander. 'Annapolis. Visiting cousins.'

He stares at the screen. 'That's near Washington, isn't it?'

'Err, yes.'

He throws specs on papers. 'Strange as it may seem, I want your help.'

'That's not like you.' I swallow a second Digestive to soothe my nerves.

'Look, you've won on Randolph Studios. Can't say I admire your tactics, but I'd have done the same. Now the game's all changed.'

'How so?'

He leans back, interlocks his fingers. 'Well, I'm damned sure you realise your shares are now worth a packet... but then again, only to us. The sooner we act, the less you'll make. Maybe you'd be kind enough to come up with a reasonable figure?'

'You'd buy me out?'

'Let's say, I'd *consider* it.'

'And what was the favour?'

'We want you to represent us at a Telecoms Think-tank, in Sydney. But never mind, I'll send Tone. He'll jump at the chance.

Oh, that sucks. 'But...' If I go to Sydney, I'll *never* deliver a plan to Brad.

He cups hand to ear, 'You were sayin', Moonbeam?'

'Thanks for thinking of me, but you'd best send Tony.'

He shunts himself back to the screen. 'I'm always thinking of your interests. Hope you realize that. How you getting' back?'

'By Tube.'

'My driver'll take you. Can't have you mixing with the *hoi poloi*.'

'That won't be nec...'

'Vee, ask Jim to run Ricky back to Pinner, will you? '

'Camden,' I correct him.

Ginger's head peers over the screen. 'My memory!' he laughs, 'I'll be callin' you Fiona next.'

Outside Berkeley Square, a black limo draws up. Jim, the chauffeur, bounces out, opens the passenger door. Once seated, I pour an orange juice from the drinks' cabinet as we head up Park Lane.

I feel guilty that I'm happy.

I play with my First-Class bed seat, as the 747 cruises to Washington. Press a knob, the seat elongates, legs tilt, backrest lowers. Then my jacket sleeve catches in the mechanism. It jolts back and forth, makes me feel sick.

'Oh dear, we have got ourselves in a jam, haven't we?' says the flight attendant. He leans over me, releases my sleeve. 'Another cappuccino?'

I'm concerned Ginge'll discover I've put my 'holiday' flight on the corporate credit card. I'm relieved the transaction won't show on my statement for a few months. By then, Brad will have let him in on our project.

'Business or pleasure?' Customs study my passport mug shot. He types into a terminal.

'Business.' I respond.

'What business?'

Special assignment. 'Randolph Corporation.'

He stops typing to inspect me, 'That's the Randolph Studios guy. You actually work there?'

'No, a sister company.'

'How long is your visit to the States?'

'Overnight.'

He stamps my passport, staples the green landing card to the inside. 'Have a successful trip, Sir.'

The next morning, I wander into breakfast at a hotel within walking distance of Dulles Airport runway.

A young restaurant manager, dressed all in black, stands at a pedestal display – *Please wait to be seated.*

I've slunk away to meet Fiona's godfather.

'I'm meeting Mr Fotherington,' I inform her. She makes a note in a blue daybook, then says, 'He's over there.' She points to an old buffer in thick tweed, slurping coffee from a mug. Bloated face, gold-rimmed monocle on a black neck chain. Spotted red handkerchief sprouts from his outside breast pocket. Completely bald, except for a ring of silver above his neck and ears.

'Mr Fotherington?'

He slams his mug down on the table. Coffee spills onto his jacket. 'Damn!' Upper-class English. He extracts a handkerchief, dips it in a water jug, dabs jacket, rises rocking the table.

'Don't bother to stand,' I say. The old fossil slumps back with relief. Sweat beads form on his forehead.

'Terribly sorry, old boy,' he says, 'not what I was.'

'I'm Ricky Stern, Mr Fotherington.'

'Let's dispense with formalities, shall we? Call me Eli.' He offers a fleshy paw.

'Ricky,' I respond.

He peers at me through his monocle. 'Fiona gave me an entirely false impression of your physical attributes.'

Charming.

His monocle falls into his lap. 'Don't take it personally, young man. You'd never make it into the Army, that's all I meant.'

'Luckily, I'm a pacifist.'

A Korean waiter hovers. Eli barks his order: 'Poached eggs, crispy bacon, fried bread, tomato, mushrooms, more coffee.'

I order brown toast and coffee. The depressed waiter scribbles, departs.

'You're not what I expected either, Eli.' I remark.

He leans closer. 'Coming from you, do I take this as a compliment or an insult?'

'You're so English.'

'I am English, you idiot! You couldn't possibly imagine I was a Yank.'

'Fiona told me you advised the last Administration.'

'Wife's a Yank. Got a green card jobbie. Her family, they're American aristocracy, Mayflower, Mothers of Invention.'

Time to move the conversation on. 'Has Fiona told you of my quest?'

'Certainly. I have a paper for you to read.'

He inserts his monocle, extracts a fat document from a beaten-up brown satchel. It's entitled 'Frankfurt Group Fundraising – Competition in the local loop.'

I scan it eagerly, find a complete overview of the U.S. telecoms regime.

'This is exactly what I'm looking for. It would take me months to produce such a comprehensive document.'

He wipes egg off his mouth with his serviette. 'Jolly dee!'

I try to hand it back to him but he won't take it. 'Keep it, it's yours,' he says.

'Are you telling me Frankfurt Group are raising money to do what we at Randolph are contemplating?'

'You're certainly quick off the mark, Stern!' Not sure if he's being sarcastic.

'Doug's the founder of the Frankfurt Group. His biographical details are on the back cover.

Douglas Frankfurt was President, Engineering at a Baby Bell phone company.

Eli clears his throat. 'They're looking for funding. I'm on a success fee.'

'How much funding?'

'An initial 100 million dollars.'

Heck. 'I can't guarantee...'

'Present it to Randolph, that's all they ask. Randolph has a problem, Frankfurt's the solution.'

'Do you want something in writing from us?' I ask.

'Fi tells me you're a man of your word...'

'Thank you.' I blush.

I'll be a hero in my own land. Or crucified.

I fly back from Washington and hide in West Hampstead. I'm supposed to be on my States holiday and can't chance being spotted. The first morning's a nightmare. I ensconce myself in our living-room with my papers, but there are constant interruptions. Gossiping cleaner, burly plumber, chatty neighbour, 'Oh, hello, thought you were away. Susie around?'

At lunchtime, Susie brings Seth home from his nursery, with a posse of four-year-olds and mums. I decamp to the library and pour over the Frankfurt Group Business plan.

It's an ideal report. Complex and detailed on the technical side; lightweight and expensive on marketing. A deal with Randolph will provide marketing expertise and lend credibility to them. I bombard Doug Frankfurt with questions via email. How, when, where? At the weekend, I sneak off to Kenwood House Café and type an Executive Summary, entitled: *An Alternative Telephone Company for America Prepared by Ricky Stern and the Frankfurt Group.* I'll ask Meg to fax it to Brad.

We watch a repeat of *Frazier* in the living-room. Seth's gone to bed. Exhausted Susie hugs me in the TV light. 'You look pleased with yourself. Was it taxing drinking tea at Kenwood?'

'I was writing an important report for Brad.'

'So important you couldn't spare ten mins to run Seth to nursery this morning, give me a break!'

'Don't get bitter.' I turn up the volume control. There's no peace for a rising young executive like *moi.*

She pokes me in the chest, 'At least Dad sold his carpet business, which let you off the hook! It strikes me this Randolph stuff's gone to your head.'

'Don't be daft.'

Yes, Commander Stern, you're with Randolph Corporation, we've reserved the best table.

We hear Seth crying. Susie pushes me off the sofa, 'Go, on. It's definitely your turn, I'm shattered.'

Monday morning, I return to the office from my feigned holiday. An unknown fat Commissar, black uniform, medals, stripes, gold buttons, has commandeered Reception.

'Pass, please, Sir.' He holds out a plump, hairy hand.

'Don't you know who I am? Where the fuck's Des? 'Pass?'

I extract my Randolph Corporation pass from my wallet, hand it to him. He raises it to eye-level, squints. 'This won't do, Sir. You need an RPC pass to enter the premises.'

'Do you know who I am? I'm the Boss.'

'You could be Mary Queen of Scots, for all I care, Sir. To enter unescorted, you will need an RPC pass. Strict instructions.'

I'll get Brad to sort him out. 'This is mad. Is Meg in?'

His boxer face is expressionless. 'Would that be Ms Walters, Sir?'

'Yes. Call her, please!'

'And you would be?' He holds a pencil ready.

'Stern. Ricky Stern.'

He writes *Stern* on a pad, picks up the phone, 'There's a gentleman, name of Stern in Reception, says he works here...' He replaces the receiver. 'She'll be right down. Take a seat, Sir.'

'What's this?' I point to a new red sofa, '...and where's my plastic Ring-Inn telephone?'

'Removed last week, Sir. And may I say that sofa is a vast improvement.'

Meg flies into Reception, clasping a Polaroid camera. 'Sorry, love, it all happened suddenly, they need a picture, smile!' The Polaroid whirrs and vomits the damp print. Slowly, my face appears, glum, dazed, pissed off. 'I'll laminate it.'

'Can I go through, now?' I ask the Commissar.

'Certainly, Sir.'

He buzzes the inner door open. I enter in a rage with Meg trailing behind me.

'What they do to Des?' I ask.

'Gave him 100 quid, told him to bugger off. He's probably drinking himself to death in an alley.'

I turn left into the main office. 'Ricky... I wouldn't... Too late!' she exclaims.

'Good God!'

Completely revamped, blinding white emulsion walls, Monet lily pond prints, chrysanths.

A complete stranger sits at Gary's desk.

'What *you* doing at Gary's desk?'

The super-confident, lanky youth, in a tight-fitting dark suit, beams. 'You must be Ricky. I've heard so much about you. How-do-you-do?' He offers thin, limp fingers. 'I'm Sebastian Hazle-Thwaite.'

Ridiculous name. 'Where's Gary?'

He grins. 'On gardening leave.'

'Gary doesn't have a garden.'

'While his severance terms are agreed.'

I turn to face a new Oriental girl. 'Hello, Ricky, remember me?'

She wears a white silk blouse, jade necklace and has silky hair. 'I've never seen you before in my life, where have you hidden Gary?' I peer over her shoulder.

'Gary's gone, Ricky. I'm Holly Wong. We met years ago at the Electricity Commission High Flyers' Conference.'

Faint recognition dawns. 'Good heavens.'

Her face commiserates, 'This must all be a big shock for you.'

An understatement. 'Did you manage to revolutionise the Chinese Electricity Supply Industry?'

'I went to INSEAD, met Tony and Sebastian. I've been working with Sebastian at Randolph HQ in New York. Tony seconded us here to kickstart the marketing department.'

That sod Tony fired all my staff and replaced them with puppets. What about Tessa?

'Let's go to your office, I'll make you a nice cuppa,' says Meg.

Meg's desk has been moved to the right of Tony's glass-fronted office. At least Tessa's still at her desk. She hands me a slip of paper. *Welcome back. I report to Holly… for now. Help! T x.* I hide the note in my shirt pocket If he fires Tess, I'm off too.

I race into Tony's office. 'You're back, Ricky. Chat?'

Meg brings in my tea. 'Want anything, Tone?'

'No, I'm fine,' he points to an Evian bottle. His office is immaculate, not a paper out of place. The weekly executive report lies open on his desk. He leans back, hands behind his head. He's grey and wasted. Jet-lagged from his Sydney trip? I pull up a chair from the round meeting table.

'We've finished the Executive Meeting,' he says.

'Finished? It's nine o'clock.'

'8 a.m. from now on.'

'8? Have you gone mad?'

'No need for you to attend, Ricky. Thought I'd field it for you in future, give you a weekly update.' He's freezing me out.

'Very kind,' the bastard, 'but I'll come from now on. Listen Tone, I was away one week. When I returned, the doorman refused to let me in. And you've fired my best management.'

Tony replies smugly, 'There are ten Stern families in Annapolis. That's where you were, right? I rang them all. One said he had a cousin called Ricky in London, but wasn't expecting you.' Snide, two-faced, bumptious, conceited, upper-class twit. I want to inform him that I'm working on a top-secret mission for Brad. That would wipe the sneer from his mug. 'Then Basil drove down West End Lane on his way home and swears he saw you coming out of West Hampstead Library.'

Whoops! Must have been my double. 'Couldn't you have waited until I got back?'

'Des was a disgrace. Gary is a freeloader. Ginger wants action. You'll enjoy working with Seb and Holly.' He sits up in his chair, raises one finger. 'This whole place needs a ruddy shake-up.'

Can't stand much more of this. 'Let's talk when I've cleared my thoughts.'

'Anytime,' he throws me a patronising grin. 'Must be difficult for you, losing your baby.'

As I leave, Meg says, 'You OK, love? You're as white as a sheet.'

'Not feeling too bright, must be the shock.'

'Meg, can you kindly accompany me to my office?'

Pass Tessa at her desk. 'You're very casual,' I remark.

'Oh these?' She points to her torn jeans. 'I'm moving around the corner. I love Camden. Maybe we could grab a coffee sometime?'

It's not time for fraternising. Especially, I've begun to fantasise about her. 'Sure,' I reply.

I rip off her dusty clothes, fling her on the carpet.

Meg follows me into my office. The door thuds shut. She cackles, 'You have a conquest there.'

'Tone probably let her stay, providing she snoops on me.'

Meg plonks down on my sofa, stretches her toes. I sift through the stack of letters on my desk.

'Can't understand why he didn't chop me,' she says.

'Too dangerous.' I reply.

'Don't get it,' she sighs.

'They can't afford to rile me too soon. I own part of the business, but they'll elbow me out. Sebastian and Holly'll nab my clients. Plus, they'll have to buy my shares. It'll all take time. How long before you retire Meg?'

'Two years.'

'Lucky you!'

I pull my summary of the Frankfurt Report from my brief-case. *Prepared by Ricky Stern and the Frankfurt Group.*

I retrieve a discarded Ring-Inn envelope from my bin, write Brad's private fax number on it, stuff my report inside. 'Take this to the copy centre in Parkway, get them to fax it to this number. When you've finished, put the envelope back in my top righthand drawer.'

'Yes, Ricky.' Meg clasps the missive faithfully to her bosom.

'That way,' I point to my secret squirrel exit down the fire escape. 'Any problem, ring my mobile. Don't use our switchboard.'

She tucks the package under her arm, flings open the Fire Escape door, charges through it, bangs it shut.

As I pass Tessa, 'Coffee?'

Holly sits at her desk, eyeing us suspiciously whilst pretending to look at an invoice.

Tessa and I stroll to Olympic Café. I'm shattered. We sit at a green mottled plastic table. She unbuttons her blouse. I glimpse brown, freckled skin. We order two cappuccinos. Around us, teenagers with tattoos, streaked purple hair, fags, listen to chart hits on a jukebox, eat chocolate eclairs.

My mobile rings, 'Hello?'

It's Meg. 'Rick, I'm in the coffee shop but there's no fax.'

'I said the *copy* shop, not the coffee shop!' I terminate the call. 'You can't get the staff these days!' Tessa giggles. I continue, 'How did you survive the cull?' I watch her pour sugar from a swizzle stick.

'I think Tone fancies me,' she grins.

'You interested in him?'

She stirs her coffee. 'Not really.' She looks into my eyes.

'How you getting on with Seb and Holly,' I ask, trying not to get distracted.

'They'd rob their Granny if it meant promotion. I can't stomach Randolph politics.' She's about to touch my hand. Thinks better of it, withdraws.

'Tony pissed me off firing my staff. Don't trust him one inch.' I confess.

'He's envious. He wants to run his own show one day.'

A punk couple with rings in their noses are snogging. 'I wish I'd chosen somewhere less gross!' I whisper. She leans towards me, her hand close to mine.

'I like it here, it's funky, but you look so uncomfortable.' She laughs.

My mobile rings again. 'Yes?'

'It's Meg. Ricky, don't kill me.'

'What's up?'

'I popped into Bar Spagna for a croissant, accidentally left the envelope there. I rushed back, but it'd gone.'

'So, you didn't fax Brad? Plus that was my only copy of the report.' It'll take me days to get it again from Eli. 'Wait a minute Meg, Spagna is right next to Phoneworks. For all we know he might have been behind you in the queue...'

'Ummm, well, actually...' Meg mumbles.

'Meg, Meg, Meg... I'm speechless...'

'I'm so sorry.' I'm fucked.

'I move in unseen ways,' says God.

I dump my mobile back on the table.

'Ricky,' says Tessa, 'you look ghastly pale.'

'An emergency. I must get back. Thanks for the fun chat, see you in the office.'

I stumble to my feet in moonlight, slip on carpet. My bedside clock, specs, glass of water hurtles to the floor. I land on my behind, 'Ouch!'

Luckily, the glass hasn't broken, but water spreads across our Afghan rug.

'Good God, what you up to?' cries Susie. She turns on her bedside lamp. 'It's 5.30 a.m. Don't you ever sleep?'

I flounder around, throw my flannel dressing gown over the water, replace the clock and don my specs. 'Sorry, young Tone's moved the Monday meeting to 8 a.m.'

'Why didn't you stop him?'

'I'm not sure if I'll attend them in future. He's offered me a weekly update.'

The phone rings. I pick up the cordless. A voice whispers, 'I'm not making this call.' Why's Fiona ringing at this time? 'They're going to fire you. And I *didn't* introduce you to Eli. I *didn't* call, that clear?' Click.

I try to explain to Susie. 'That was Fiona. She says she didn't introduce me to her Godfather and she didn't just call! Can hardly ring up Ginge, and say, 'Hi, old boy. Fiona didn't tell me you were firing me.'

'No, you can't.' replies Susie.

'Guess, I'll have to carry on as normal.'

'You haven't been forging more Honours, have you?'

'Don't be daft.'

She holds me tightly. 'I don't like those awful people. They're only interested in how much money they make.'

'Steady on.'

'Well, all this Brad Randolph nonsense... you're like a naïve schoolboy.'

What nonsense? Brad's my mate. He'll sort things out.

'Got to go to the meeting. I'll call if anything disastrous happens.'

I finish dressing, kiss her goodbye, creep out the front door without waking Seth.

Seated in my company Mercedes, I realise Fiona wasn't warning me, she was protecting herself. Why fire me? I was carrying out Brad's instructions. True, I didn't tell Ginge, but Brad warned me not to. I drive into my Camden office forecourt. If they've fired me, I'll be locked out.

Tessa skips down the entrance steps in a black trouser suit, flat black shoes. Her hair's tied back, teeth gleam in the early morning sun. She says Tone's sent her out for coffees.

I enter our building and reach inside my breast pocket for my pass.

Sorry, Sir... instructions to escort you from premises... We'll pack up your belongings, forward them to you. Now, please leave quietly, we don't want a scene...

'That's fine,' says the portly Commissar.

There's excited atmosphere in the Boardroom. Tony's at the head near the door. Sebastian and Holly either side. I hesitantly sit next to Sebastian. Basil enters and after serious consideration, places himself next to

Holly. The turncoat wants to ingratiate himself with Tone, distance himself from me. Tessa returns and hands out refreshments. Coffee smell fills the air.

Tone's flagging. His body in an untucked cream shirt lounges back. Six o'clock shadow.

'What time you get in this morning?' I ask him.

'7 a.m.' he replies. 'Been going through management accounts with Baz. Before that, had an early catch-up breakfast with Ginge.' Did he mention firing me?

Who's betrayed me?

Sebastian and Holly beam at Tony. Tessa flashes me a cute smile. Baz scours through figures.

Let he who is without sin...

'Ok, troops,' Tony enforces silence. 'Our first priority is to provide the Group with a taxonomy.'

'I agree,' barks a bright-eyed Sebastian in a check suit. 'What do you think, Ricky?'

'Non parlo la lingua administrazzione,' I reply. Everyone looks baffled.

'It's a joke,' explains Basil, all nasal.

'Is it, Rick?' asks Tone.

God help me. 'I don't speak management jargon, Tone. What's a taxonomy?'

'We need to classify what business we're in.'

'The pleb Phone business!' I reply.

'I think we're New Media,' says Holly. She runs a biro through her short brown hair.

'Content business,' says Sebastian.

Tessa sips coffee, glances my way.

'We'll need a special session to iron this out,' says Tony. 'How am I fixed tomorrow, Tess?'

She produces a hand-held organiser from a slim case, flips it open, prods it with a metal pick. 'You can do 7.30 a.m. or 6 p.m.'

'Let's do 6. We'll work 'til the job's done.' A flurry of electronic diaries. 'Can everyone update their Outlooks? Holly, the restructuring?'

Holly pokes her Palm Pilot. 'I'm preparing a memo. Shall we call it redundancy?'

'Oh, that won't do,' replies Tony. 'Downsizing, right-sizing, delayering or rationalising.'

'I like rightsizing,' she scribbles onto her Palm Pilot with a metal spike. 'We'll also need to motivate the remaining staff. I propose a herogram programme.'

'Brill!' says Sebastian.

'A herogram?' I scoff.

'Yes,' explains Holly, 'every month, we'll highlight one of our outperforming staff.'

'I like it,' says Tone. 'Well, I'm timed-out. We've still got to fine-tune the outsourcing programme, but I've a slot at lunchtime. Let's reconvene then.'

That evening, I fling my jacket over a kitchen chair, loosen my tie and trouser belt. I draw a heart on the steamed-up window and help myself to penne.

'Good day at the office, darling?' asks Susie, ironically.

I tip penne onto a plate and join her at our white folding melamine table. Seth is bolted into it in his blue plastic, Bloomingdale's baby seat. His mouth oozes tomato soup, which runs on to his pale blue bib. I sit a safe distance away and spoon mashed potato from his plastic Mr Men dish. He closes his mouth as food approaches.

'Here let me!' Susie drops her knife and fork, takes the spoon, feeds Seth. He burbles and kicks his legs. The radio plays a jazzed-up "Over the Rainbow".

I stuff pasta into my mouth, swallow. Pull a face at Seth who squeals.

'A taxonomy pre-meeting. Didn't even know what the bloody word meant.' I hate going to the office, to meetings. I hate arse-licking and plotting. I had a different plan of how to do business. Now I'm one of *them*...

'What business are they in?' Susie raises her eyes, tuts.

Highlights of the day flit into my mind. 'I endured a CAPEX review committee, a staff memo-drafting meeting, a herogram selection sub-committee and a budget review.'

She downs Seth's spoon, hands him a plastic dinosaur. He covers it in tomato sauce and chews it. 'So did they fire you?'

'Not a squeak.'

As if on cue, the phone rings. I run into our bedroom and grab the cordless. 'Hello?' I return to the kitchen, cradling the receiver to my ear.

''Ello me old China!'

'Ginge?' My privacy has been invaded.

Seth emits a high-pitched yell. 'Feedin' time at the zoo? We need to chat, Moonbeam. Tomorrow at 9 a.m.?'

The end is nigh. 'Sure, I'll be there.' I rest the receiver on the table, stare at Susie. 'Looks like tomorrow will be the *finale* at Randolph Corporation.' I feel terror and relief. No more meetings means no more money.

FINALE

22

I stroll into Ginger's office. He taps on his tidy desktop. 'Sit!' he orders. Sweat trickles down my back. I pull up a chair from the vast meeting table, park myself by fresh freesias in the vase between us.

He shoves his phone and table lamp to one side, snarls, 'Tell me, Sunshine, one reason why I shouldn't fire you on the spot?'

'For what?'

He grabs a piece of paper, 'According to this... here... read it yourself.' Fax on Phoneworks notepaper, dated 12th May 1998:

Dear Mr Randolph,

Yesterday, I was visited by Ricky Stern, CEO of RPC. He expressed dissatisfaction with your organisation and outlined plans for a U.S. project. He asked whether Phoneworks would be interested in backing him. I kept a copy of the plan and said I'd get back to him.

Needless to report, we have no confidence in Mr Stern, but would be pleased to co-venture with Randolph Corporation. Whilst writing, we have many ideas for maximising the profitability of RPC and would be pleased to discuss these with you at your convenience.

Yours sincerely, Matthew Grabball, President, Phoneworks.

'And this, too.' He hands me a copy of a fax from Brad.

Addressed to Ginger, it reads: *'Sort Stern. Dump Him? Brad.'*

Brad's pissing on me from a great height. And I loved him. 'You believe Grabball? That criminal toe-rag?'

He leans back and opens his arms wide. 'I'm gullible... wanna defend your honest self?'

Truth time. 'Brad warned me to tell nobody about developing a States plan.'

He points at me. 'That's why you told Grabball. He's nobody?' He laughs cynically.

'I didn't tell Grabball. My assistant Meg left the file in a coffee shop by mistake.'

'Aha....' He doesn't believe me. Even I find this difficult to believe! 'And how did you know about Frankfurt?'

'Someone introduced me to Doug Frankfurt via an intermediary.'

He produces a red cardboard file that contains a report. Licks his thumb, flicks through. 'Aha! Eli Fotherington.'

I stare at the file in horror. The buggers have been tracking me. 'Is there anything you don't know?'

'I'd prefer to hear it from the horse's mouth.'

'Eli gave me the plan. I précised it. Instructed my assistant to fax it to Brad. She left it in a coffee shop by accident – as I just told you. When she tried to retrieve it, it'd vanished. She confessed that Grabball was behind her in the queue.'

He nods in disbelief. 'Wow! Old Camden's full of spies, is it?'

'Grabball's obsessed with my success. He's an unscrupulous bugger.'

'I presume you had no idea Ms Fiona was on a kickback from Frankfurt?'

Oh, God....

'No, I didn't.'

'She and Fotherington would get $50k each.' Crikey. 'We backed the plan on condition they hand their bribes back. Your mate Fiona Wallace resigned without compensation. Brad met Frankfurt last week, liked him. He once admired you too, but now look.' He holds up the fax. 'Dump him?' he jabs the offensive word. 'Rotten come-down for our resident genius, eh?'

'And now?'

He grimaces, swivels his chair, places his legs on the desk. 'Brad's got it in for you, Sunshine. You're fired!'

'What?'

'What is it about fired you don't understand? It's over, curtains, kaput. We're going to pay you half a million fuck-off money. That's for your remaining shares.'

'But that's nothing like I'd make from Randolph Studios alone...'

'Listen, my friend, be grateful we're not dismissing you for breach of bloody contract. We'll send over the papers for you to sign to your house tomorrow. Now clear off. Go back to your office and clear your things. Another concession – letting you back there. But from tomorrow you're B-A-N-N-E-D! Now get out!'

I stagger out of his office.

Veronica approaches with a tray in hand. 'Gosh, that was a quickie! Want your tea out here?'

'No thanks Vee, need to get some fresh air...'

I glare at Brad's inflated image. 'Thanks a million, buster!'

'Well, half a million,' says God.

I stagger into Berkeley Square, sit on a bench, breathe deeply. Try to make sense of what just happened. I've been fired but I'm now wealthier than I ever thought possible. Brad's a man of his word, so the money will be in my bank account by the weekend.

At least I'll be able to make Susie happy. Send Seth to that posh alternative school up the road. The one where kids are meant to be happy rather than crammed full of useless facts.

Then remember Grabball. He bloody won. That bastard. Start another business, just to compete again – win this time?

'Are you bloody mad?' says God.

Can't bring myself to call Susie yet. Need a plan.

Feel hungry. It's 10:30 a.m. Didn't have time for breakfast. Head through Berkeley Square towards Maison Bertaux in Soho. Tea and one of their croissants. Opened in 1871 but I've only been visiting since the 1980s!

Walk past Selfridges. Mum still shops there every Christmas, I mean Chanukah. Then past the Cumberland Hotel. Met my first girlfriend there at a Jewish Youth Club tea event.

Don Smith comes to mind. Why I am always surrounded by Jew-haters?

Snap out of it Stern. Get a grip!

Along Old Compton Street, into Maison Bertaux.

Owner Michelle greets me. 'Hi Ricky, it's been ages.'

'Hi Michelle. Yes, I've been busy at work. Gallivanting around the world...'

'Lucky you! Someone was asking for you. About 10 minutes ago. He said you'd likely be popping in.'

'What? Who, how? Did he leave his name?'

'Nope, sorry. Said to tell you The Englishman called.'

Baffled, I go upstairs, grab a table, wait for my order to be brought up, stare at the mirror engraved 'Liberte, egalite, fraternite.' Not a lot of that about these days...

There's a family finishing their breakfast next table. Down from up north. Dad, Mum, 10-year-old daughter. Must be a half-term break.

Dad looks anguished, stares at the bill, 'Oh, no. I don't have enough cash. Better pop out to the bank.' He rises, clutching his wallet.

I have cash. I've just been promised half a million quid. 'Let me treat you. I've just come into some money unexpectedly...'

'No thanks!' stares at me like I'm a pathetic wanker, shoots out. Mum and daughter are embarrassed. 'Sorry about Bill,' says Mum and turns her eyes to heaven.

Michelle appears with my tea and croissant. 'He's here. Wants to pay for your breakfast.. what should I tell him?'

'This is just too odd Michelle. Sure, let him pay. Why not? I smile at Mum, who looks even more embarrassed.

'Did you see what I just did?' says God.

I'm about to answer when a hand appears. 'Chop!'

Don Smith sets himself down opposite me. Plonks his coffee cup on the table, spilling its contents into his saucer. I stare at him in amazement, shake outstretched fingers half-heartedly.

'Don't look so dejected Shylock. You're a rich man... If I were a rich man...' he starts singing.

'Don, how on Earth did you know I...'

'Don't concern yourself with trivialities...' he replies smugly. 'Come eat up, you've got a meeting to go to...'

I wolf down my croissant, he downs his coffee, gets up. He's put on weight. Wearing linen suit, striped blue shirt, Club tie. Can't make out the club name. Probably cricket. The tie knot dangles at half-mast.

He staggers to his feet, stomach about to explode from his shirt.

'Bye Michelle,' he shouts. Michelle stares at him puzzled and shrugs her shoulders. Blows me a kiss.

He leads the way at an impressive rate of knots and soon we are at Holborn and entering Lincoln's Inn Fields. The homeless encampment has been cleared and rehabilitated. There's a café there now.

We enter GRAPE offices. There's a pile of boxes in Reception. Copy of *Siddhartha* sticking out of one. Suddenly the penny drops. They've cleared my Camden office!

The Reception guy sits at his desk. Neat black uniform, cap, vaguely familiar. Suddenly he recognises me, jumps to attention, shouts 'Guv!'

Des, what are you doing here?!'

'Kind Don Smith,' points at an impatient Don, 'offered me a job when I was fired from Camden...'

'Enough jabbering, come Ricky we'll be late,' shouts Don.

Don plods up 3 flights of stairs with me in tow to the meeting room, enters and collapses in a chair around the Board table. And opposite him sits Holly! She's immaculately dressed in a handmade white trouser suit. Beautiful Chinese eyes stare at me inquisitively. 'I brought your things over from Camden in case you want to stay. If not, I'll get them to your home.'

'But what are you doing here?' I ask Holly.

'Oh, that. Don asked me to join the team a few weeks back. He said his dad, Ken, put in a word for me.

Apparently, Ken received good feedback from that conference you and I were on together. Tony let me go easily enough. He just seemed pleased to cut overhead.'

'Cut the crap. Where's the boss?' Butts in Don.

At which point who should walk in but Terry Tomblin smirking. 'Top of the morning to yer Ricky me lad. I've missed you.' He hugs me, seats himself at the table and beckons me to the chair next to him.'

'What on Earth is happening Terry? Have I died and not noticed? Aren't you in Oz? Is this the Afterlife?'

Don smirks, 'No Afterlife for you matey, not after what you did to our Saviour...' Holly half-suppresses a smile.

'Don't tell me you're the boss, Terry.' I stutter.

'Me?! You out of your mind? Too busy with me racing commentaries, newspaper articles...'

Suddenly Matt Grabball walks in, looking debonair and handsome and sits at the head of the table.

'Chop Boss!' Don points gleefully at Matt.

I shoot up, 'Right that's it. I'm out of here. Don't want anything to do with that bastard.'

'Steady on Ricky. I'm about to explain. Make you an offer you can't refuse,' says Grabball in a calm, steady, voice and almost kind look I've never seen before on him. 'Tell him, Don.'

Don takes over, 'When you joined GRAPE, we wanted to test some new technology in the field and we thought you'd be a good... well how can I put this kindly... sucker. Didn't you ever ask yourself how with your complete lack of qualifications, you gained a vast salary and an entry to British Embassies? You see I'm all heart, Groucho.'

But hang on Don. You joined GRAPE when I did. You were working at the Lewisham Electricity Showroom.'

'Lewis who? That one of your kosher mates?'

Terry continues, 'Remember Hamish at that weird retreat Susie sent you on?' I nod. 'He suggested the phone idea and recommended me, right? Well, he's one of us...'

'One of what Terry?'

Terry smirks enigmatically.

'But wait a minute, what about the bugging? How did *that man*,' pointing at Grabball, 'know everything? Leonard removed all the bugs.'

'Oh Ricky,' Terry puts his head in his hands. 'And who recommended Leonard? We wanted to give The Boss free reign, to see what you were made of.'

Terry cuts in, 'We simply replaced Green Fingers with... well I'd better not say more.'

'Des, Tessa, Gary... YOU?'

'You know I can't say...' replies Terry lamely. He's clearly embarrassed.

'Look, Terry. This is all too much. Just tell me why I'm here. GRAPE fired me. Why on Earth should they want me back?'

Grabball actually deigns to speak. 'Did we fire you?'

Don scoffs. 'You sure this moron's up to the job? You resigned Einstein. Do you have memory loss now to add to your many other faults?'

Grabball chimes in. 'OK, you fucked up but if it hadn't been for that ditzy PA of yours, you might still have a job with Brad.'

'But my time with Brad. Was that all a set-up too?'

'No', replies Grabball. 'We could see from the very beginning you'd never survive there. But you made a packet on the way, right? What's not to like? And anyway, now I'm best mates with Brad, thanks to you!'

'I know I should never have trusted you. Grabb-all. I mean that says it all!' Now I'm getting petty!

'That's not my real name, you idiot. I dreamed it up. People will believe anything!' says 'Grabball.'

'Actually,' chirps in Don, 'I was at Uni with Bev Grocock...'

'Was she a looker?' enquires Terry.

'Let's move on,' Matt's getting irritated now. 'Terry, tell him why he's here...'

Terry speaks, 'We want you to rejoin GRAPE. We think you've now got... well, almost got what it takes. Would you like to be based in Tel Aviv, working out of our, I mean the British Embassy there? We've got a new product. Anti-virus. Stops all those nasty people out there tracking you. Know what I mean? Wink wink. We'd pay for a nice apartment, babysitting from the in-laws. Move that ex-con Des there too to look after you. Fat salary to add to your gigantic payoff from Brad.'

I cut him off mid-flow.

'This is all too sudden. Can I go home now and think about it overnight? I obviously need to discuss it with Susie.' I get up, shake his hand, 'Chop' to Don, kiss Holly on both cheeks, reluctantly shake hands with Grabball. He smiles benignly. 'Des will order you a car home. We'll call you.'

As I approach Des, he stands to attention yet again, says, 'See you in Tel Aviv, Guv? Cab?'

'Sit down Des. I'll let you know tomorrow. Now I'm walking home, I need some fresh air.'

I exit the building and head north, thinking about my options. Relocate to Tel Aviv and start again as a Senior Salesman on a whacking great salary? All that disruption but in-laws on tap. What could possibly go wrong?

'You'll see,' says God mysteriously.

ABOUT THE AUTHOR

Born into a traditional Jewish family in the fifties, East End of London, and expected to go into the family optical business, Stephen developed an eye phobia that freed him to pursue his own path.

Following graduation as a computer scientist from Manchester University, he worked as a computer programmer. Consumed by boredom, he resigned and attended a 4-month Transcendental Meditation (TM) Teacher Training course. On that course, he had an unexpected 'calling' to go into business, despite his lack of relevant experience. Instead, he was inspired by his grandfather, an inventor and semi-professional tap dancer! Needless to say, he only taught TM to a handful of folk yet still retains a keen interest in meditation and spirituality. His 'calling' led him to many adventures in the business world: founding five London cable TV companies, several TV and newspaper competitions using premium rate services for the first time, possibly working for British Intelligence by accident and eventually selling his business to a media mogul.

He has been writing short stories for decades and finished *Wild Card* 20 years ago based on his business adventures, though fictional, of course. Stephen's previous publications are *Enlightened Business* and *The Authentic Entrepreneur*. He lives in Richmond, Surrey with his wife Luiza and together they travel the world inspired by Luiza's wanderlust.

https://stephenkirkorg.wordpress.com/

www.ingramcontent.com/pod-product-compliance
Ingram Content Group UK Ltd.
Pitfield, Milton Keynes, MK11 3LW, UK
UKHW011347200525
5986UKWH00004BA/369

9 781036 915308